BONDED
TO THE
BEAST

INTERNATIONAL BESTSELLING AUTHOR

SARAH SPADE

FOREWORD

Thank you for checking out *Bonded to the Beast*!

This is the third book in the **Sombra Demons** series, a set of interconnected standalones that tell the stories of the human women who stumble upon the *Grimoire du Sombra* that holds the 'true love' spell that summons their mates, and the shadow demons fated to adore them at first sight.

If you haven't read the first two books yet, that's okay! Each one is designed to be read on its own, in any order, and all you have to know going into this book is that Kennedy—the heroine of *Bonded to the Beast*—is the bookseller that sold the spellbook to Shannon—the heroine of *Mated to the Monster*—in the first place. Obsessed with it for reasons she can't understand (yet), Kennedy is ecstatic when Shannon brings the book by her shop—and that's where this story begins.

Her hero, Loki, is also a bit different from previous Sombra demons. When they first meet, despite his intentions to seduce her and make her his mate, he definitely earns the title of 'beast' if only because they can't communicate and he comes across a bit caveman-like after their initial mating. That's because he's not just a demon; he's fully demonic, lost to the shadow side of this shadow monster. In his head, you see he's as devoted, possessive, and protective as Malphas and Nox are once he has Kennedy as his mate. It just takes a little time before *Kennedy* knows that.

Written for readers 18+, this book has: mentions of past infidelity (Kennedy's ex is garbage, and she's much better off with her beast), the captive romance trope (since Loki kinda steals her without her consent when they can't communicate), instalove, explicit sex scenes & profanity, and the breeding/pregnancy trope.

Touching on that last one, it's been established in this series that mating on the night of the gold moon basically guarantees that bonded couples will get pregnant—and in this book, like in *Santa Claws* (the Shannon and Mal holiday novella), the heroine finds that out… and while it's not a surprise to readers or the hero, it definitely was for both Shannon and Kennedy ;)

Enjoy!

FOREWORD

xoxo,
Sarah

PROLOGUE

LOKI

ONE HUNDRED YEARS AGO

Though few will admit it, every Sombra demon fears going fully demonic.

It doesn't happen often. Most of us are too honorable to lose control in a way that makes us no better than the monsters that lurk on the edge of Sombra's shadows—unless, of course, we *become* them.

Just like I have.

The banishment to Nuit should have been enough to stop me in my madness. Being forced from the School of Mages, banished to a small village built on Sombra's far-flung ash fields, that should have been enough to learn that patience is a virtue.

That anything worth having—worth *keeping*—is also worth waiting for.

It was not. It did not.

And now, with my hands clasping my aching head, claws digging into my cheeks, both sets of my horns stabbing wildly as even the pain can't stop me from jerking my head... the madness has taken hold of me.

The madness, and the *rage*.

That's what did it. That's what made my purple gaze fade to blinding white, my words little more than snarls that barely drown out the pounding in my skull as I lose complete control of the male I once was. The rage made me demonic, while the missing mate I crave drove me wild.

It's all my fault. Even as I stumble from the home I conjured with the promise of my female in mind, I know that the only one I can blame is myself. Sammael warned me that there were some spells a mage should never cast, but I thought I knew better.

But I wasn't thinking like a scholar. I was thinking like a lonely male who was willing to take any risk to find my mate.

I don't know if Sammael guessed that I stole the matefinder spell from the archives in Marvo. My mentor made it clear that, while magic runs our realm, there is only so much it can accomplish. Courtesy of the shadows that make up our second form, we have no control over finding our fated mates.

At least, not with Sombran magic. Either my female will find me, or I would have to travel this plane and all the others to search her out. It's the trade-off the gods gave us. We are immortal, powerful, *strong*, but we're tied to one true mate and it's never easy to find them.

I refused to believe that because I was different. Born with a set of double horns, the mark of a powerful demon, I was convinced that my magic would be enough to call her to me. Whether she lived on Sombra or Soleil, a neighboring plane where most Sombra males find their females, I wouldn't spend another three centuries hoping to chance on my forever.

Sammael even admitted that the spell might have worked in ages past. Before Duke Haures closed off our realm from fabled worlds we talk of as if they're legends, the magic was stronger. Now, the parchment with the spell was a relic of its time, and not to be trifled with.

Oh, but I trifled. As I dig my feet into the ash, swallowing a pained howl as my head throbs and my chest feels like it's been ripped open, I can still feel the echoes of my soul splintering when the spell backfired on me.

Because I searched for a mate that I cannot reach, and that, more than anything, is what has broken me.

I'm lost. Alone. Even as the members of my clan peek their heads out of their homes, watching as I drag myself out of Nuit, I am completely apart from them. I'm too dangerous to stay among the clan that welcomed me when Sammael caught onto my obsession—and possibly my theft—and sent me away from Marvo. No longer the honorable male I once was, I've fallen prey to every demon's fear.

There is nothing left for me to do.

I'm more beast than male—and the cruelty of it all is that I recognize that. Feeling as though I'm being pulled toward a mate I just cannot touch and every part of me wanting to rip the worlds apart to find her, there's only one place for me.

And that's where I go.

In the distance, just past the ash fields of Nuit, the shadows on the edge of Sombra beckon me. I'm still sane enough to know that I must abandon the village, and I push forward until their oppressive weight welcomes me.

Glowing eyes, the same white shade as mine now, watch me curiously… *hungrily*… from every corner of the darkness. I fear them not. I still have claws. I still have fangs. Both are longer, sharper as I struggle to retain my demon form; already my shadows beg to join the darkness surrounding me. There are prey beasts here, and predators that could challenge a Sombra male, but I'm a two-horn.

Worse, I'm a two-horn without any essence to remind me who I am—and who I was.

The shadows should fear *me*.

Still clutching my head, I stumble over the horned skulls that cover the ash-covered ground. The warmth of Nuit fades. The shadows are cooler than the rest of Sombra, and without the gold moon to illuminate it, the black moon takes on the colors of the inky shadows suffocating me.

Something scurries by. My nose scents meat, though I haven't hungered since the spell failed. If I do, I'll have to hunt for myself. Provide for myself.

Of course. I'm all alone now, and I have no one else to blame.

There'll be no bartering in the shadows. Any demons who survive long enough to make it their home are like me: fully demonic, and unable—or unwilling—to be part of a clan. We're all alone, and with the magic inside of me weakened by the shadows, I'll have to do everything on my own if I want to exist long enough to meet my mate.

Because that's all I have to live for, and all I've ever wanted. For three centuries, I hungered for her. To know what it was to be loved, to be touched, to fill her with my seed and be there as we rear our offspring. To share my essence, to accept hers, to be the best male I could be... all that I could have had if I'd just waited.

Why didn't I wait?

I shall wait now. I shall claw my way through every day, lurking in the darkness, hoping for the moment when she'll favor me with her body, her heart, and her essence.

And, gods willing, I'll have a drop of my own to give her in return.

Because, even as I give in to the urge to throw back my head and roar to break up the eerie quiet of the watching shadows, I know that the only thing that will save me from my terrible mistake is my fated female calling me to her. Summoning me to her side. The mate bond snapping into place could heal the fractures of my soul, replenishing the essence of Loki, her mate's promise finally banishing the shadows that have taken root inside of me.

Until then, I belong to the dark. To the shadows.

And should they take me before my mate can find me? It's no less than what I deserve for thinking she wasn't worth waiting for…

CHAPTER 1
GRIMOIRE DU SOMBRA

KENNEDY

I knew that I was in trouble when I started thinking that a little B&E might not be such a bad idea.

I was sitting on my towel, sprawled out on the sands of Point Pleasant beach, staring at the waves rolling in even though my thoughts were back in Jericho, New York.

The chill from the ocean meant I'd left my swimsuit back at the hotel. Instead, I had a t-shirt and a pair of capris on, idly wondering if I should just cut my trip short so I can start planning my new life of crime as I dragged my finger through the damp sand.

The beach was mostly empty. Technically, it wasn't open yet. Memorial Day weekend marked the opening of the Jersey Shore and I was a little early. It was the only week I could get away from my bookstore, though, and I'd desperately needed the vacation when I planned it back in January.

Then again, that was before I started obsessing over an antique book…

When I first sold the old leather-bound book a few weeks ago, I was just glad to get a good price for it. I teasingly told my customer that the *Grimoire du Sombra* —seriously, that was the name printed inside of it— was a spellbook. I didn't really mean it, and I'd bet that Shannon didn't actually believe me, either. But she gave me fifty bucks for it, and if she wanted to think it was an old magic book, that was fine with me.

But then I started to think about it. The big, brown book would pop into my brain without warning.

At first, I thought it was because I might have been able to get more for it if I had thrown it up on eBay instead of selling it at the store. I mean, I like money. That was why I couldn't stop thinking about the stupid thing, right?

Yeah… when I started to actually *dream* about reading it, even a book lover like me had to admit that I was being kind of weird—and that's nothing compared to my brilliant idea of sneaking into Shannon's apartment and stealing it if only to figure out why it seemed to have cast some kind of spell on *me*.

What worried me even more is how that actually seemed like a much better idea to me than, I don't know, maybe asking my customer if I could buy it from her?

That's what a clear-headed, non-obsessed, *normal* woman would do, right?

Of course, if you ask my ex, I'm none of those things. And, in his perspective, it's also the reason we're exes.

In my perspective, it's because he was trash and I'm better off without him.

And, no, I'm not bitter that he ended things after so many years together. For the last five or six of them —ever since I opened up my little shop on Main Street in Jericho—we were more roommates than lovers anyway, and I was almost expecting it when it was over. Blaming the demise of our relationship on my obsession—*ha!*—with books and my stubborn need to run Turn the Page on my own without any staff or any of his help, Tyler decided that he didn't want to be second to my store any longer.

Fair enough. Honestly, he could've left at any time and, while it would've hurt, I would've understood.

But he didn't leave. Oh, no. He just started an affair—

No. That makes it sound nicer than it was. What Tyler really did was start fucking my younger sister, Hallie, behind my back. Twenty-eight to my thirty-two at the time, she was my shadow when we were kids and my best friend a decade ago.

Now I haven't spoken to her, Tyler, or my parents

in two years, planning a solo trip to the New Jersey shore was the highlight of my last six months, and I ruined it by pretending I was Carmen freaking Sandiego or something, plotting how to steal a book instead of hitting the clubs and getting laid for the first time since I found out Tyler was sticking his dick in my little sister.

That's what I had planned to do during my trip. I'm still holding out hope for Mr. Right, but I would take Mr. Right Now just to scratch this itch I have.

This is the longest I've been single since I started dating in middle school. I might not have been *in* love with Tyler anymore, but our break-up sucked. I had planned my whole life around that asshole. We were going to get married. Tyler and me... we hadn't set a date yet, but after dating for eight years and being engaged for three, it would've been sooner than later. Kids would have finally come next, little footsteps pattering around the backroom of my shop, giggling as they toppled over stacks of stock I hadn't put out yet.

That dream died a fiery death two years ago when I ran upstairs to the apartment during a shift at the store and found Tyler plowing Hallie in our bed.

So shocked at what I found, I remember throwing one of my heels at his back. When he yelped, jumping off of her, my other heel got Hallie right in the forehead as she sat up, already trying to explain.

How could she? Like, were they both naked and

he somehow tripped and fell into her vagina?

Please.

I didn't want to hear it, either. Returning to Turn the Page in my bare feet, I sent Tyler a furious text that I expected him to get the fuck out of the apartment before closing—and that was right before I impulsively went online and bought a new mattress to replace the one upstairs.

That was the last time I saw either of them face to face, and boy did it take a lot of rosé to burn *that* out of my brain.

Still, sometimes I do wonder if Tyler decided to dump her when—*gasp*—she hit her big 3-0 in February or if they're still together. I have no way to know. When my parents told me that I should want my ex-fiancé and my sister to be happy, I went no contact with all of them.

Pretty easy when I spend nearly every waking hour in my store, and not one of my family members ever gave a crap about my business.

Besides, Kennedy always does what she has to to survive. She moves on, even when it seems like it's impossible.

And when she gets her mind stuck on something, she's like a dog with a bone only even more tenacious.

I hadn't taken a vacation since Tyler heeded my unsaid threat and packed up all his shit by the time I closed the store up that fateful night. I might look delicate and sweet, with a heart-shaped face, a gentle smile, and a seemingly innocent expression… but I have a temper. He knew that better than anyone.

I'm also super stubborn. Throwing myself into work, I would prove to him—prove to all of them—that I didn't need to be in a relationship to be happy. He always accused me of loving my store more than him anyway, and maybe he was right. I settled for him because he said he wanted kids and, apart from Turn the Page, it's always been my dream to have a big family of my own.

Now Hallie is living the life I once thought I wanted, and I can't stop thinking about a *book* of all things.

I didn't regret selling it until a couple of days into my vacation. By then, I'd already done a few searches online, hoping I could find another copy of the *Grimoire du Sombra*; if not, then at least some information on it. I guess when I told Shannon it was one of a kind, I was right.

I don't know why I'm so drawn to it. The embossed pentacle on the cover caught my attention when I found it thrown into a box of stock I bought from an estate sale I went to one night in Connecticut, but except for reading the strangely formatted title page written in an unfamiliar language on the inside, I didn't get a real good look at it before I sold it to Shannon.

That was probably my mistake. If I'd flipped through the pages, maybe tried to translate some of it, there's a chance I'd have already forgotten about it like I do every other book I sell.

But I didn't, and I haven't.

All I remember about it is its title, and while I already knew what a grimoire was—hence me telling Shannon it was a spellbook—I had no clue was a Sombra was. Google failed me on that front, too. Somehow I doubted the book had anything to do with a video game from 2016 or a brand of topical pain relieving gels, but those were the first results that came up when I looked.

So, you see, that's why I thought stealing it seemed like a brilliant idea. When I couldn't even explain to myself why I felt like one particular book—of the thousands I've sold over the years—called to me over all others, how could I bring it up to one of my best customers without looking like a lunatic?

With the seagulls cawing over my head, I did eventually manage to talk myself out of stealing it from Shannon. After wasting so much of my life with Tyler, I could kiss my hopes of ever having kids and a man who actually loved me for me goodbye if I got thrown into jail for a little breaking and entering and some petty theft. I would just have to wait until the right time to see if maybe Shannon would be inter- ested in letting me buy it back.

Even if I *did* end up cutting my vacation short.

Instead of staying through Sunday, I decided to go home late Friday night. And while I could blame it on the rainstorm that came through the shore town or not wanting to miss out on any weekend sales, I know the truth. Shannon likes to stop by on Saturdays when she's off work, and even if she doesn't stop by my shop, odds are she'll go to The Beanery for her daily latte. I can flag her down there.

That was my plan. It was a good one, too, and I resigned myself to waiting until I saw Shannon. I was banking on her visiting Turn the Page. One of my most loyal customers, the snarky yet friendly blonde usually came by every couple of weeks to check out my new stock.

I could wait. And maybe by the time I see her again, I'll have gotten over this ridiculous need to get back the old book I sold her.

I *could* wait—but, as it turns out, I don't have to.

———

Turn the Page follows a similar set of hours as the other shops that line Main Street. We open every morning at ten, close at six, and I work all shifts, Sunday through Saturday. Along the stretch where my store sits, there are only two establishments that open before ten: The Beanery, the coffee shop next door, and Sal's, a deli that serves bagels in the morning and sandwiches for lunch.

My first day back, I almost decided to stop by Sal's for an onion bagel with cream cheese. By the time I arrived back in Jericho last night, I was too beat to restock my fridge; whoever says that some folks need a vacay from their vacay got it right with me. I barely had enough energy to unpack and do a load of laundry before bed, let alone go grocery shopping.

But then I thought about how much work waited for me after a whole week off. Instead of the bagel, I popped into The Beanery to grab some coffee and a croissant. It would be quicker, and I'm thinking I'm going to need the caffeine. Especially after last night's sleep… and how little of it I got.

Notably, for the first time in days, I didn't dream of myself in my shop, leafing through the same leather-bound book that's been haunting me lately. Instead, I had the strangest… I don't know. I don't want to call it a nightmare exactly because I wasn't scared. The opposite, actually, since I woke up with my hand inside of my panties.

I can't tell you the last time I had a sex dream. Ages, but what made me so unsettled when I woke up wasn't the disappointment that I was alone in bed. It was the memory of the faceless male who was stroking me reverentially in my dream as I rubbed myself in my sleep.

Male's the right word for it. He wasn't a man. He was more a *monster*. Huge and muscular, with a dick to match, I couldn't help but think he was *in*human.

And I would've blamed it on the alien romance series I'd been working my way through on my Kindle while on the beach if it wasn't for the fact that dreaming about the shadow man touching me... it was like coming home for real.

Like greeting an old friend I'd somehow forgotten about.

Before I got with Tyler, I would have dreams just like that one occasionally. Always with a hulking male figure that was hidden in the shadows, who looms over me while caressing my body as if I'm precious. He never speaks except to grunt as he touches me, kisses me, *fucks* me. Not sure what it says about me that my dream guy keeps his mouth shut, puts my pleasure first, and hides in the shadows so I can't see his face, but it was a welcome change from obsessing over that stupid book.

Even if the glimpse I got of my shadow man last night had *horns...*

Lucky for me, a cold shower washed away the lingering heat rushing through me when I dragged my weary and aroused body out of bed. By the time I was pulling the door open to The Beanery, all I was thinking about was whether I wanted the plain croissant or the chocolate-filled one for breakfast.

The Beanery is bustling. Nearly all of the tables are filled this morning, and the three baristas behind the counter are rushing back and forth. Tasha is handling all of the food, Lisa Ann making the drinks, and Derek is on the register, taking orders and passing drinks and pastries over to the customers.

I join the line, checking the time on my phone. I have fifteen minutes until I have to open the shop. With this crew working like a well-oiled machine, I'll be unlocking the door with plenty of time.

Before I know it, it's my turn.

"Hi, Derek."

Derek works most mornings at the coffee shop. He's cute, almost reminding me of a puppy. He's got these big brown eyes and soft curls the same shade. A couple of years younger than me, he's a friendly guy that I've gotten to know courtesy of my frequent trips next door.

He smiles at me. "Hey, you! I thought you weren't going to be back until Monday."

Me, too, Derek. Me, too.

"What can I say? I guess I missed Jericho too much."

"Or your bookstore," he teases. "So what can I get you this fine Saturday morning? You want your usual?"

Large coffee, no milk, six sugars. "That would be great. And a chocolate croissant if you still have them."

"Warmed up?"

"Yes, please."

"No problem." He enters my order into the register, calling out, "Chocolate croissant, Tash. Hot."

"On it!"

"Okay, Ken. That'll be $7.12."

Derek is the only one I've ever met who calls me 'Ken'. Sometimes I think the boyishly handsome barista is as charming as *he* thinks he is, but whenever he uses that nickname, I almost want to ask him if he's seen Barbie around somewhere.

I can't stand it, but after how disappointed he looked the first time I corrected him, I let it go. Besides, I'm an old pro at keeping my grin from wavering, concealing my feelings when I have to. That comes from being the disappointing oldest child, I guess, or maybe it's because of how most people— even strangers—treat me as way more innocent than I ever was because of my appearance.

Besides, something else he said caught my attention. My 'usual' he called it. And while, yeah, that's definitely my usual order, it reminds me how I'm not the only repeat customer The Beanery has.

After tapping my debit card against the card reader, paying my bill and adding a couple dollars' tip for the baristas, I glance over my shoulder. No one's joined the line behind me.

Good.

"Hey, Derek?"

Because he also noticed that the rush had died down a little, he grabbed a large cup and started pouring the coffee in, helping Lisa Ann out with my simple order.

His eyes flicker up at me as he fills it. "Yeah?"

"I've got a question for you."

"Shoot."

"If I give you the name of one of our locals, could you tell me if you know them?"

He finishes with the coffee pot, setting it back on the warmer. Bringing the cup over to the counter, he reaches for a lid and a handful of sugar packets. "Sure. Who is it?"

"Shannon Crewes." I remember her last name from her credit card and when Derek doesn't give me a weird look, I figure he might have expected something similar. "She shops with me a lot, and I'm pretty sure I see her in here from time to time."

Derek chuckles as he snaps the lid on my coffee. "Time to time? If it's the same Shannon I'm thinking about, she gets her morning latte like clockwork."

That's just what I was hoping to hear. "Do you know if she was in today?"

"Not yet, but it's Saturday. She usually comes in later. Though, that reminds me… hang on." He passes the coffee over to me, and when Tasha comes up behind him with my hot croissant in a paper bag, he nods at me.

She holds it over the counter. "Here you go."

"Thanks." I take the bag and the coffee, watching curiously as Derek digs around one of the drawers behind the counter.

"Ah ha!" Slamming the drawer shut, he holds up a—

I tilt my head. Is that a scrap of receipt paper?

"I can't believe I almost forgot. She was actually asking about you the other day. Something about a book?"

My heart nearly stops. "She was?"

"Yup. She wrote her number down and asked me to pass it along to you if I saw you before she did. What a coincidence that you were asking about her just now." He holds the scrap out to me. "If you hadn't, I would've totally forgotten about that."

Coincidence, huh? Maybe. Maybe not.

I take the slip of receipt paper with Shannon's number on it, folding it in my fist. I try not to let my excitement show as I pick up the bag with my croissant in it again.

"Thanks. I'll have to give her a call and find out what that's about."

"No problem. Have a good day, Ken."

I tighten my fingers around the scrap and offer Derek a smile way more genuine than the one from before. "You, too."

It's five to ten by the time I juggle Shannon's phone number, my coffee, my croissant, and my keys in order to pop the lock on Turn the Page. After turning the lights on behind me, my first instinct is to set my breakfast down, grab my phone, and call Shannon right up.

Then I remember how Derek said Shannon didn't usually stop by The Beanery until later on the weekend. The last thing I need is to blow any shot of getting that book off of Shannon by waking her up early on a Saturday and having her pissed at me.

Patience, Kennedy. Open the store. Get the registers up and running. Check your e-mail.

Do your job.

Tucking Shannon's number underneath my cash register for now so I don't lose it, I get to work.

One thing I can say? It was a good idea to come back early, no matter why I did. I have plenty of customers to keep me occupied all morning to the point that I'm still nibbling on my croissant during lunch. I shut down for fifteen to grab a ham and cheese from Sal's because I'm still hungry, then return to dive into a box of stock I meant to put out before I headed to the beach.

By the time I actually have a moment to call Shannon, it's late afternoon and the perfect opportunity to find out just why she was looking for *me*.

Taking a deep breath, filled with nerves I can't quite explain, I grab the slip of receipt paper out from under my cash register, punching it into my phone.

It seems to ring forever before—

"Hello?"

"Hi. Is this Shannon?"

"Sure is. How can I help?"

"This is Kennedy. Kennedy Barnes. From Turn the Page? When I stopped in to get my coffee this morning, Derek gave me your number and said you were looking for me…"

CHAPTER 2
WHITE CHALK

KENNEDY

As much as I needed the week off, there's so much I have to do now that I'm back.

Invoices to pay, orders to make, stock to go through… and I'm not doing any of that anymore.

Instead, pacing behind the narrow cashwrap, nervously playing with the skirt on my sundress, I'm watching all of the passersby on Main Street, willing the little bell over my door to jingle as it opens.

I thought I handled the phone exchange pretty well. After I confirmed that the book Shannon had a question about was *the* book I've been dying to get my hands back on, I offered as casually as I could to buy it from her if she no longer wanted it.

If only it was that easy.

She didn't want to return it or to sell it back. Instead, she wanted to ask me where I got it from.

It seems as though the book snared her attention as much as mine. And while I couldn't answer that question, I did take the opportunity to ask her to bring it in so I could "double-check" for her.

Shannon said she would. That was about half an hour ago, and I haven't been able to focus on anything else since.

A customer would be a great distraction right about now. Of course, with my luck, it's no surprise I don't get a single one after I hang up with Shannon— which is probably why I jolt in place when the door finally opens.

It's Shannon. She has her long white-blonde hair pulled back in a high ponytail, her toned arms on display courtesy of her tank top. As she waves at me, I notice the large sunflower tattoo on her upper right arm before my gaze is immediately drawn to the over-sized, leather-bound book she's got tucked at her side.

"Hi!" I hope my smile isn't too deranged. I fist my hands to keep from snatching the book from Shannon. "I didn't expect you to stop by so soon."

Because, yeah, my luck's *never* that good. I might have invited her to bring the book by so that I could get a look at it, but I never expected her to drop what she was doing to take the walk over from her apartment.

Even if I'm stoked that she did.

Shannon's one of my best customers. From our frequent conversations as she's milling around the store, looking for another off-the-wall romance to buy —like me, she loves them—I learned that she lives in one of the apartment complexes a few blocks away from Main Street. Also like me, she's perennially single, but she calls it "in-between boyfriends" while I'm sitting here, waiting for the "one" to make me forget all about Tyler.

Of course, unless he's a reader and he finds his way to Turn the Page, I'll probably be waiting forever…

After exchanging some more pleasantries, I realize that Shannon is as happy to hand the book off to me as I am to take it. Meeting me at the cashwrap, she hefts it onto the counter, sliding it across it to me.

A spark shoots through my fingertips the second I touch it. In an instant, I know that this was meant to happen. I was meant to get the book back.

Now I just have to figure out a way to keep it.

Shannon raps her hands anxiously on the counter as I pick up the book.

"So," she says, "what do you think?"

Though I already know the answer, I scan the barcode sticker I had slapped on the book when I first realized it didn't have one. Like I told her on the phone earlier, some of my stock has to be inputted into the POS with a dummy SKU. A way to ring it up at whatever price I think it deserves. I usually reserve that for out-of-print books that aren't in the system, or books so old, they don't have a UPC printed on them.

The worn leather of the book's binding had put it in the second camp. There was no copyright page with any of its printing information, either, so while I have no idea when it was first bound, its yellowed pages and embossed cover scream "tome".

Or, like I teased the day I sold it Shannon, a "spellbook".

The scanner beeps, but just like I expected, there's no information coming up on my screen. Not that I would have told her if there was, but it's better this way. After all, I've never been a good liar or an actress.

Oh, no. That was all *Hallie*.

And while I admit that I might have ulterior motives when it comes to this book, I am telling the truth when I say, "I'm sorry, Shannon, but I guess I sold this to you before I put it in the system."

Her shoulders slump. I have no idea why it matters so much to her where the grimoire came from, but I feel bad when she's visibly disappointed.

I feel bad—but it also gives me one hell of an idea.

Tapping my fingernails against the embossed cover as I continue to hold it, I tell her, "But, if you want to leave this behind with me, I can make a couple of calls, show it to some members of a group I belong to. Someone might recognize it, and if not, I can see if I have anything else like it in my inventory."

"Um. Yeah. If it'll help, that's okay with me."

"It won't be long," I promise. Just long enough for me to figure out why this book means something to me, and for me to get over it. "Maybe a week or two? Then I'll have this right back to you."

"Okay."

Shannon's gone from disappointed to distracted as she turns her head, looking behind her as though she expects to find someone else there. Weird since we're the only two in the store, but after I suggest she check out some of the new romance books I put out earlier, she nods and wanders off.

She doesn't stay long. After a few moments where she meanders down the racks and rows and piles of books I have everywhere, I get the idea she's searching for some*one* and not a new book to read. I try to keep up the chitchat when she comes back to the counter empty-handed. Last thing I need is for her to change her mind and take her book back with her.

Thank the Lord, she doesn't. Only half-listening as I mention that the book might have come from one of the estate sales I'd stopped by, she cuts me off with a 'thanks' before waving goodbye and heading for the front door.

I've never been so glad to see a customer leave without buying anything before in my life.

I HAVE THE BOOK.

A giddy little giggle escapes me as I hug it to my chest. That went a lot smoother than I ever expected it to, and for one of the first times ever, I decided to go ahead and close the store down early.

I do wait about five minutes after Shannon left before I shut off the lights and lock up. Too eager to dive into the grimoire, I don't bother counting down for the night. I can do that later, or just add it to the deposit tomorrow.

Tonight? I want to see what this book is all about.

My cozy apartment is directly above my shop. I make one exorbitant rent payment for both spaces, and while I'm just squeaking by at the end of the month, it's worth it to have a bedroom, a bathroom, and a small kitchen within walking distance of my job. I don't even have to leave Turn the Page to go home if I don't want to. Behind a closed door in the backroom, there's a flight of stairs that leads me right into my cramped living room.

Kicking off my heels once I get upstairs, I head right for my bedroom, lugging the heavy book with me. From the moment I accepted it from Shannon, I've been buzzing. The little hairs on the back of my neck are standing on end, goosebumps running up and down my arms.

Am I making too much of an old book? Probably.

For all I know, I've got goosebumps because I left a window open in my bedroom and it gets chilly at night. It doesn't matter. I can't wait to crack this baby open.

Plopping down on the edge of my bed, I heft the book onto my lap. That's when I finally notice there's a receipt peeking out from the top of the book. It's shoved in the middle, and it looks just like the type of bookmark Shannon would use.

Looking closer, I notice it's a receipt from The Beanery.

Oh, yeah. Definitely Shannon's bookmark.

Hmm. If something about this book has Shannon asking questions about it, the page she marked might be a good place to start, right?

Letting the book fall open, I almost choke when I see what kind of "spell" it lands on.

On the top of the thin, yellowed page there are two words printed in a heavy block typeface: **VERUS AMOR**. Right beneath the print, someone used a pen to write a translation in script: *true love*.

A true love spell. You have got to be kidding me.

Only… I think someone actually took it seriously. I don't think it was Shannon, either; the handwriting looks old, the ink from the pen somewhat faded. But the translation isn't the only addition to the page.

I don't even know where to begin. There are drawings in the margins, sigils and another pentacle like the one on the cover of the book. Instructions, too, including one that says:

Before you cast the VERUS AMOR spell, it's important to draw the protective sigil (illustrated below) in yellow chalk. That done, draw a circle in salt around the sigil.

Um. Okay. Might be nice if the author said *why*. I mean, if this is a 'true love' spell, why would I need a protective circle? That doesn't make any sense to me and, oh God, I can't believe I'm actually buying into this.

Does that stop me from reading further?

Nope.

I run my finger down the page. There are two distinct passages in print. Overall, I haven't the foggiest idea what language this spell is written in. It's like a mish-mosh of a few different recognizable languages and then some random letters thrown in for good measure. I recognize 'cuore'— 'heart' in Italian —and obviously 'amor' is love, but 'tiernyg' and 'druggul'? Even a quick Google translate comes up with nothing.

The passages aren't translated like the name of the spell, but the first one has the word 'manifest' scrawled next to it. The second one is starred, marked as 'promise'.

Interesting. Very interesting.

I tap the page. My fingernail underlines the instructions.

I'm thirty-four. Too old to believe in fairy tales and

happy endings, especially when my Prince Charming turned out to be a two-timing villain. I should know better than to think magic is real, or to believe that I can read some foreign words and I might actually manifest my true love.

Then again, thirty-four isn't *that* old. I still watch cartoons a lot of the time because they're fun, and my favorite dinner is a bowl of Cheerios with milk and sliced bananas when I don't feel like cooking. I might not believe in fairy tales, but I've held out hope that the "one" for me might be out there somewhere.

Maybe I just need to do a little magic of my own first to find him.

Yellow chalk, huh? If I'm going to attempt this—and, for some reason, I have this feeling like I'm *supposed* to—I need chalk. Salt, I have, but chalk?

Hmm.

THE ONLY STORE I COULD HIT ALONG MAIN STREET before it closed was the local dollar store. It didn't have any colored chalk, though. Just packs of white.

I bought one, and a small thing of salt in case my kitchen was low on the stuff. It might not be perfect, but I figure it's close enough.

Because I don't have the yellow chalk, I take a lot of care copying the sigils in the book to create the protective circle that's on the page. I end up using my bedroom floor to draw with the chalk and sprinkle the salt. It made sense. My apartment has hardwood floors, though the living room has a rug stretching across it. It was either the bedroom or the kitchen, and… I don't know. True love. Bedroom. It just seemed right.

By the time I'm done, my knees are killing me from all the kneeling and crawling around I did. I ended up running out of salt and using most of the extra container I bought before the circle was complete.

That done, I get to my feet, brushing my chalky, salty hands off on my skirt as I eye my handiwork.

Looks good, I decide, then turn back to the book.

The spell seems simple enough. Once the protective circle is done, my next step is to read the first passage.

That part is not so simple.

I stumble over the foreign words, getting frustrated when I'm not sure how to pronounce them, but I do it and—

—absolutely nothing happens.

I wait a couple of seconds, glancing around the room as if expecting someone tall, dark, and handsome to suddenly appear in the middle of the bedroom. Nope. For good measure, I read the first passage again, in case my pronunciation was so bad, I messed up the spell.

Still nothing.

Just like I should have expected.

Snorting, I slam the book closed. My fault for getting my hopes up, as though the gibberish I read would actually do anything. I don't really know what I thought would happen, but whatever it was, it probably wasn't worth the mess I'm going to have to clean up now.

As I leave my room again, heading out to grab my dustpan and broom—and a wet rag to mop up the chalk—I have to shake my head.

Who knows? Maybe I should have waited until I had some yellow chalk after all.

CHAPTER 3
HUNT

LOKI

I've been tracking the arkoda for three cycles of the gold moon.

Of all the beasts that lurk in the shadows, it's the only one who has ever eluded me. Not because it is wily or because it is a better tracker and hunter than I. I've already proven that it was not when I trapped one once before. It was a brutal hunt, but I was victorious, and I had meat to last for a full cycle once I butchered the beast with my claws.

In the shadows, it is eat or be eaten. We are all prey in the dark. You must want to be the one who survives the most. My demon instincts beg that I do. For one reason, it is because I am immortal. If any of the other beasts bested me, they could feast on my flesh for centuries. My shadows would ensure that I forever regenerate unless I'm weakened in some way. By enchanted chains that bind my shadows and my essence perhaps, or by going fully demonic and finally giving up on this existence.

Like I almost have.

Even as I stalk the beast, I must admit that I have grown weary of this life. When there is nothing to exist for except making it through another cycle, time slows. I know not how long I've hunted the dark, only that I continue to wait for the only thing that will give me purpose—and the second reason why I refuse to let the shadows completely take me even after all this time.

I wait for her. For my female. I hope for her with every breath while also knowing that I shall never likely have her.

How would I? Unless my demoness is as lost as I, she will never appear in the shadows to find me. She might be crossing over Sombra, maybe even visiting from Rouge Brille or Soleil or any number of demon planes, longing for her male, but Loki is here. As though I've always belonged in the chill and the dark, I can't bring myself to leave.

There is plenty to eat. In the small two-room shack I conjured before the last of my magic fled me, I have a bed I rarely use, a tub I long ago turned into a store for my meat supply, and a water tube so that while I hunger for my female, I don't suffer from thirst.

I guard my home fiercely, hunting any prey that dares approach. Skulls line the outside. Most of them have horns, the remnants of Sombra demons of eons past who begged for death from either our ruthless ruler—or the arkoda.

There is one I prize for how different it is. The skull had no horns, a smaller head, and bones that belonged to a creature unlike any I've met in the shadows.

In my madness, it called to me. Though I did not hunt the creature it belonged to, I carried the skull home like a prize, tossing it in the corner of my resting quarters.

Perhaps I am meant to search the shadows for other such strange beings, hunting them for meat and to protect my claimed territory. I thought that once, when I first found it many cycles ago, but I've never seen another since.

And then, of course, my obsession with the arkoda began.

Three heads higher than the tallest Sombra male, with thick shadow fur, glowing white eyes, claws designed to rend, and fangs that would snap off my solid arm in one bite, the arkoda is a fierce beast that has the ability to consume the shadows themselves. In either of my forms, it's a worthy opponent, but the one I chase is more than that.

It is the mate of the female I defeated four cycles ago. Even bigger and more ferocious, the male is intelligent enough to know that I am the reason he has no female. Wary that he will meet the same fate, he does not attack me, but he lingers on the edge of my territory, taunting me to face him at the same time as his presence frightens some of the easier meat away.

I do not fear him. If my fate is to succumb to the arkoda, so be it. Maybe then this endless torment of wanting a female who is a whisper in my mind and a dream whenever I do sleep will finally be over. It's worth the hunt, and should I survive as I have done for ages, then I will prove once again that Loki and his two-horns are more powerful than anything the shadows have to offer.

Once I was full of rage. I am not now. More mournful than anything at what my arrogance and eagerness has cost me, I've spent my time in the shadows learning to be patient.

That is why, when I'm closing in on the arkoda's newest nest, I force myself to ignore it when my instincts tell me to turn back. As though something is pulling me, tugging me, it reaches for the essence of Loki—and, yet, there is still none to find. As demonic today as I was when I allowed the shadows to swallow me whole, I have not been able to recover any of it.

Without my mate, it does not matter. Without the essence, the strange sensation that I'm being called is a mere buzz in the back of my skull. The arkoda marks his nest with a fervor that has my nose wrinkling. I'm so close to finding the beast, and I'm eager to end the hunt at last.

It's him or me, and I'm not sure who I want to be the victor.

———

WILY BEAST. LEAVING HIS DROPPINGS BEHIND AND A disturbed nest, I thought I found the arkoda's lair.

I did not. It was abandoned, and I headed for my shack with a snarl and a fresh ungez for my supper.

Unlike the arkoda, the ungez is small and simple. It does not take much to hunt the creature. Friendly as they are, they will hop into a hunter's grip, offering themselves up as a meal. For a male my size, it's little more than a nibble, but with the arkoda continuing to elude me, it's all I have this night.

I'm thinking about whether it would be worth it to gather some of the roots that grow in the shadows and stew my supper rather than eating it raw when I miss the step in front of me. That is not usual. The shadows are dark, but my sight is keen. I know the land surrounding my shack as well as the ridges over my nose. I don't misstep, but I did.

Immediately on my guard, I go still. I see nothing that would have tripped me. Not an ungez underfoot, or a skull buried in the ash-covered ground. Odd. Breathing in deep, I sample the chill in the air, searching for a threat.

Over the familiar scent of brimstone that lingers even in the shadows, I take into my lungs a scent so delectable, so sweet, so *enticing* that I don't want to exhale. I want to keep it forever, bottle it up, and never let it go.

My cock agrees.

From my first breath, the scent has my cock stirring. In Nuit, it is expected for villagers to cover themselves in their solid demon form with either shadows when they expect to change forms, or woven garments when they don't. Since moving to the shadows, I'm insubstantial more than not. Regardless of forms, though, I don't bother with any coverings.

The only time my cock begins to twitch, hardening and lengthening, begging for me to take it in hand and stroke myself to release is when I allow myself to think of my mate. It isn't often, since I feel the ache of the miscast spell so strongly even now, but on lonely nights when the gold moon is high, I don't stop until I've rubbed my cock as often as it takes to remind myself what exactly I'm waiting for.

My one true mate. The female born to be mine. Who will let me mate her, love her, worship her and her forms... and then be with me forever. No longer will Loki be lonely. We shall have a home together. A family.

A life that was worth every bit of the madness inside of me.

As my cock goes completely hard, heavy and achy,

tender to the touch, I marvel at it. I was not thinking of the promise of my mate. Ungez stew should not be an arousing thought. But that scent…

That scent has me ready to mate. Not just to find pleasure as I dream of her, but my body poised to take her and make her mine.

I take another deep breath. The scent is fainter than it was, but its effect on my body is not. My heart thuds against my chest. My fingers flex, as though reaching for her. Whirling around, I search the shadows, but I see nothing.

And then that same sensation from before rushes through me. The feeling that I've been snared in a trap, that someone is calling me to them.

Because they are. After long last, it's my female.

I no longer resist the pull. Giving myself up to it, I'm not surprised when a portal appears in front of me. Impossibly darker than even the darkest shadows, it's like a hole before me, beckoning me to take a leap.

At the same time, my solid demon form shifts to shadow. Bright golden runes light up along my arms, shining like a beacon. It's magic, I realize. Powerful magic unlike any I learned when I was still studying at the School of Mages.

I cannot cast a spell like this one, but I know exactly what it is; if I hadn't been so consumed by my failed hunt earlier, I would've recognized it before. This is a summoning, and one that can only be performed by one soul.

My female.

My *mate*.

She's calling to me. Now that I understand that she's searching for her male, I will answer.

Tossing the ungez back to the ash, the shadowy creature melting into the dark around us, I give myself over to the pull.

I'm not sure where the portal will take me. Wherever it is will be off-plane, of course. The golden runes glimmering on my arms as I leap into the portal are a mark of a traveling spell that leads its wearer out of Sombra. But there are a few characters down my one arm that I do not recognize. Wherever I am going, it won't be a world that I've studied. And while most Sombra demons find their mates in our neighboring realms, there are countless that might keep my mate.

Countless—but only one that we talk of as legend.

The human realm. A fabled world full of mortal creatures who cram their entire existence into one century at most, it's supposed to have magic unheard of even to a mage. Before my obsession with finding my mate took hold, I'd often wondered if I could convince Duke Haures to allow me to further my studies in the human world.

It would not have been easy. The duke's first law makes it so that mortal worlds such as where the humans live are forbidden to any demon from Sombra. They are not to learn of our existence, and only on the rare occasion that a male is summoned by a human's magic to be their mate are we allowed to visit their world.

Unless, of course, Duke Haures sends you. One of the reasons I looked up to Sammael as my mentor was because he was the duke's personal mage. As his mage specialties involved portals—as well as the enchanted chains Duke Haures used to keep his subjects in line—Sammael had been to the mortal world before. His stories fascinated me, and though there hasn't been a demon called by a human in my lifetime, I often wondered if that fate would be mine.

If it wouldn't be, perhaps I could make it. At least, that was my rationale when I stole the matefinder spell from the archives in Marvo. If humans had the magic to summon their demon mates to them, why couldn't a powerful two-horn mage do the same?

But now I know why my spell failed all those years ago. I was searching for a mate who did not exist. Who could not.

Because my female? She's human. Mortal. She never would have been born when I cast the spell—but she must have used magic of her own to call to me now.

And, stepping out of the portal, landing in the shadows of her quarters while she slumbers peacefully before me, I have answered.

The moment I manifest in my shadow form on the other side of the portal, it winks out behind me. I know better than to try to summon it myself. Mage or not, a portal back to Sombra won't open for me from the human world. I don't have the magic my mate does, and I'm trapped in this human world until I claim my female or I release her from our mate bond.

She's mine, and I will do anything I must to make it so.

CHAPTER 4
IN MY DREAMS

KENNEDY

It shouldn't be so hot in my room. It's *May*. I don't have to worry about turning on the AC until at least June.

Tell that to how I wake up shortly after I fall asleep, sweat welling at the base of my neck and beading along my brow.

I'd already kicked my blanket off, I notice. Still half-asleep, I yank off my sleep tank and my shorts, leaving me in my panties and that's it before I pass out again.

It seems as if only a few minutes pass before I'm semi-conscious. The heat has faded some. Goose-bumps pucker my skin. I grope for a blanket to wrap myself up into and as the blanket slides across my sheet, I hear something.

No. Some*one*.

It's someone sucking in a breath, the sound so short, so sudden, that I jolt up into a sitting position.

"Hello?" I call out into the darkness. It's pitch black. Just in case, I grab my blanket, covering myself up to my chin. "Is someone there?"

In response, something big shifts in the shadows. As my own breath catches in my throat, a pair of lights flicker on.

Hang on—

Those aren't lights. Twin circles standing about six and a half feet off the ground, I'm pretty sure those glowing white orbs are *eyes*.

I've seen them before. Him, too.

And always in my dreams…

I squint. As my eyes adapt to the dark, I start to pick up features in the midnight gloom. Some kind of horn arcs up and over a head as big as a basketball. The rest of the body moves in the shadows, the shape amorphous and flowing, though it seems *huge*.

There's a nose. A mouth. When lips part, gleaming white fangs appear in the darkness. Long black hair floats around the head.

I'm dreaming, I realize. This… this has to be a dream.

As I stare, the shadows flicker, then disappear, revealing—

"*Oh.*"

If this was real life, I would be screaming. But

since this is a fantasy ripped right out of my psyche, I actually marvel over my dream monster's true appearance.

His skin is a dark red, like freshly spilled blood. His eyes are still white, his nose long and pointed; so are the tops of the ears poking through his long black hair. He has slight bumps over his nose and *two* sets of onyx horns. One pair arcs over his head like a crown while the other curves inward before curving out again from his heavy brow.

His muscular form would make a bodybuilder envious. Dipping my gaze low, cooing softly when I see the cock jutting out from his hairless groin, I add that he has a dick that would put a porn star to shame.

And, tonight, he's all mine.

Glancing up again, I see that the claws on the edge of his red-skinned hand are as black as his shadows and his hair. As his lips curve invitingly, he shows me his pointer finger before slowly, seductively crooking it in my direction.

He doesn't speak. He doesn't have to. He beckons me and, still reverberating from the jolt of recognition I experienced when I met his glowing white gaze, I slowly climb out of my bed.

I inch toward him.

Impatient, my dream monster takes a few steps toward me.

Between one footfall and the next, he shifts forms

again. Going from the red-skinned, brutish-looking demon back to a shadow monster with those eerie white eyes and a vaguely amorphous shape, he outstretches his hand toward me. His black claws bleed right into his inky, shadowy skin, but when he crooks one at me again, I... I tiptoe toward him.

It's almost like I can't stop myself.

As though he's responding to this pull between us, he meets me by the foot of my bed.

He cups my jaw, tilting my head back, making me look up into his eyes. There's no pupil there. Just a solid white orb that glows like a lightbulb.

He whispers something I can't understand.

Could he be asking if I'm ready for him? Deciding that he is, I nod.

Dropping to his knees, he shoves his nose against the front of my panties. He moans deeply, his big body shuddering as though he likes my smell.

Using the edge of his shadowy claw, he slices one side of my panties, then the next. Grabbing the material, fisting it, he tugs, pulling it free.

Now we're both naked.

Rising up to his impressive height, he reaches around me. His hand curves my bare ass, leaving a heated trail wherever his shadows touch me. I throw back my head, enjoying the sensation, gasping when he lifts me off the ground.

I clutch his shoulders, wrapping my legs around his waist. I can feel his hard cock trapped between our bodies. It's as big against my belly as the monster dick I saw when he traded forms, and if this wasn't a dream, I'd be massively freaking out at this point.

Good thing it is a dream. Even better, it's another one of my sex dreams. So sex is inevitable. A dick like that would rip me apart in real life, but as hot and ready and *wet* as I am right now? He'll fit.

He has to.

"Give it to me," I murmur, shaking my hair out as he lays me down on the bed. "I want it."

Lord help me, I want this monster.

He doesn't answer. At least not with words, he doesn't. He grunts, then climbs up on the bed, moving between my open legs.

For one terrible moment, he looks down at me like he doesn't know what to do next. That can't be right. In my dreams, my monster is like an incubus. He visits me, pleasures me, and makes me realize that no human man would ever be able to compare to him.

But then he lines our bodies up, slowly feeding his cock inside of my waiting pussy, and I exhale a sigh of relief.

"Yes," I breathe out next. "Yes. This is what I want. *Yes*."

He grunts again, pushing a little more. Waiting to see if I can take it, if I can take *him*, he searches my face. I guess he's proud of what he sees because the monster smirks before shoving himself the rest of the way in.

Once seated as far as he can go, he starts slow, rocking in and out of me as though getting used to the motion. Once he finds a rhythm that feels good to both of us, he picks up speed. A few short shallow thrusts before he pulls all the way out, slamming back in, he keeps one hand on my hip.

The other inches up my side, moving slowly until he's able to palm my entire tit in his big hand. He rubs one claw against my tight nipple and I gasp. I can feel his hand on my skin, but the claw? It's almost completely intangible. Just a whisper of heat that has me just about begging for him to do that again.

He doesn't. I'm not even sure he hears my keening whine over the slap of our bodies together and his frantic breath. Above me, his face is screwed up in concentration.

Pulling out, he twists his hips, finding his way back inside of me at a new angle.

He hits the exact spot to set me off. Clutching my sheet with my fingers, the coil that had been building low in my gut snaps as I start to come.

I've barely finished when he follows right behind me.

I'm not prepared for it. Probably because I've never gotten this far in a sex dream before. Usually, right when I'm about to come, I wake up, feeling achy and unsatisfied. That he managed to get me to climax from penetration alone just proves this is a dream, even if it's not my normal one.

But for him to throw back his horned head and howl as he nuts inside of me? Can't lie, my sexy dreams are on freaking point because I've never seen or heard anything so damn hot before in my life. Like his orgasm snuck up on him and, with a masculine roar, he wants the whole of Jericho to know that he was experiencing it.

His groin is pushed flush against mine. Dreaming or not, I realize that the monster has me taking every inch of him as he shoots his load, determined not to let a single drop of his come escape as he bucks up into me.

And he's not wearing a condom.

I mean, right? Besides the fact that I'm not sure how to go about putting a rubber on a shadow monster, I don't think CVS sells a jumbo demon size.

Good thing this isn't really happening. I've never had unprotected sex before. I always told Tyler I wouldn't until we were actively trying for kids, and it was another twist of the knife when he pulled out of Hallie the day I caught them and I saw that he was fucking her bareback.

Well, it's my turn to get pounded with nothing between me and my dream lover. With his temperature being so much hotter than mine, I almost swear that I can feel him filling me up, though that could just be the sensation of this shadowy figure almost taking me partway inside of him at the same time as his dick is still parked inside of me.

Because he is. He's still hard, too. Nutting once didn't do anything to deflate his erection which, hey, makes sense. Why would I conjure up a dream lover who was a two-minute man?

Especially since I'm inexplicably attracted to his more monstrous form. He's the male I've dreamed of before, and when he shifts again, I'm gazing up at him, watching him solidify right before my eyes.

Whoa. I thought I was stuffed before. That's nothing compared to now.

He murmurs something but I'm a little preoccupied, adjusting to the new sensation of being as full as humanly possible. I feel like a butterfly pinned to a board. I don't think I could move if I tried.

I don't have to.

Cradling me in his brawny arms, the monster lifts me up by my back, shifting our positions so that I'm on top now.

That helps. I can decide the pace, rising up when I'm ready which, because I'm still dreaming, is much sooner than I ever would in real life. My body stretches to accommodate his monster dick, my cream coating the dark red length as I rise up, then let my body weight guide me back down on him.

As I move faster, turning it into a bounce, I swivel my hips, leaning forward so that my swollen clit dances over his taut lower belly.

He watches in amazement as I dip my hand

between our bodies, plucking at my clit, rubbing it frantically as I stay seated on his cock.

My pussy tightens as I come apart on top of him; at the same time, he bucks his hips wildly, my orgasm leading him to follow right behind once more. I'm not completely sure if he finishes again. Both sated and suddenly exhausted, I drop down, splaying my body over the monster.

Considering how gently he runs his shadow claws along my spine, almost as if telling me 'good job', I'm thinking he did.

And that's the last thought I have before every-thing goes black as I fall back into a well-earned dreamless sleep.

MY DREAM IS STILL FRESH IN MY MIND WHEN I FINALLY begin to wake up again the next morning.

I'm sprawled on my side, one hand pillowing my cheek, the other nestled between my naked thighs. For one terrifying second, I don't know *why* I'm naked. I distinctly remembered changing into a tank and sleep shorts before going to bed. Still half asleep, it takes a second until I recall getting so hot in the night that I stripped down to my panties.

Only I'm not wearing them anymore, either.

Strange. Maybe I got up in the middle of the night to pee and I kicked them off or something.

Considering my thighs are somewhat sticky as I flop from one side to the next, I wonder if I forgot to wipe.

Something dribbled, and since I haven't been with a guy since Tyler, it's way more likely that I had a bit of an accident than any other reason I might be sticky. Unless I got so turned on while I was sleeping I creamed myself.

If that's the case, I think I need to sign up for a dating app or something. The 'true love' spell was definitely a bust, but if I'm so hard up that I'm getting off on a sexy dream about a seven-foot-tall monster of all things, I need to get laid and *bad*.

Whatever the reason I'm sticky—sweat, pee, or something else entirely—I know that a shower is in order. Checking my phone for the time, I see that it's eight o'clock. Plenty of time to get up, get clean, change, and have some breakfast before heading down to Turn the Page.

Shimmying out of my bed, I go over to my dresser. I pull out some fresh panties, a bra, and a pair of nude stockings; to me, May is sundress and flats weather so I'll need the stockings. The shoes I can pick out after I'm showered. Since I usually get dressed in the bathroom, I'll need to grab a dress.

I keep my collection of dresses, sweaters, and jeans hanging up in the closet. That's all that should be in there.

So why, when I fling the door open, do I see a pair of eerily familiar glowing white eyes?

The way it's positioned in my room, it's always been dark in the closet. The door blocks the light from the window hitting it so the small closet is full of shadows.

Today, it's full of the shadow man I dreamed about last night.

Only it wasn't a dream, was it? Unless I'm still dreaming—

I pinch myself. Ouch. I felt that, just like I see the way his eyes glow even brighter when I let out a soft yelp.

My yelp becomes a cry of surprise when he lashes his shadow arm around my hip, dragging me into the closet with him.

What is he doing in here? Forget the more obvious question—how can he be *real*—since there's no denying the brand on my naked hip as he tugs me up against his hot body. But if last night wasn't a dream… why did he leave my bed and go hide in the closet?

Shadow, I think. He has that red-skinned form, but he's also part shadow. How much do you want to bet that he can't be out in the sunlight?

Just like how do you want to bet that the magic spellbook I messed around with last night *did* actually work? *Manifest…* oh, I manifested something last night.

Worse, I *fucked* it.

And from the way those glowing white eyes are

traveling all across my notably naked body, I get the feeling that he wants to do it again.

I don't even get the chance to back out of the closet or even try to stop him from whatever the shadow monster is planning. Letting go of my wrist, I have a second to react before he lowers both of his hands to my waist.

With an *oof*, he lifts me up easily. And I mean *up*. My legs are dangling for a moment as he raises me high over his head. Mine nearly bumps my vaulted ceiling before he shifts my weight, hooking my legs over his shoulders.

Losing my balance, I fall forward, hands grasping wildly for something I can grab onto. Pushing past the fabric and the metal hangers hooked over the closet bar, I wrap my fingers around that.

His oversized hands are holding onto my waist. He gives my ass a gentle push, scooting my bare pussy as close to his mouth as possible. His nose bumps up against the top of my mound. Something solid yet slick nudges my labia.

Fangs, I remember, bringing back some of the more hazy details of last night. This monster has equally monstrous fangs and they're *centimeters* away from my private parts.

His breath is as hot as his skin. At least a good ten degrees warmer than mine, I shudder at the sensation.

That was probably a mistake. Thinking I'm already enjoying myself, he starts to lick.

No, I think, almost hysterically, he starts to *eat*.

He devours my pussy with a single-minded yet slightly sloppy devotion that has me squirming from that first lick. Whether he knows what he's doing when it comes to a human woman's body or he remembers how I played with myself last night, I have no idea, but he makes sure to circle my clit in between nuzzling my pussy and dipping his tongue into my entrance.

He murmurs something that comes out muffled. The vibration makes me moan. Taking heart in the noise, he does it again.

Oh my God, that feels amazing.

He nuzzles again. Nips, though he doesn't use those monstrous fangs of his. Sucking my labia into the heat of his mouth has me digging my heels into his back. Still in the inky black shadow form, they pass through the first half-inch surrounding him before I find something tangible.

Once I do? I spur him like he's a freaking horse until I end up riding his face to an orgasm so power-ful, my scream echoes around the closet.

When my legs finally stop shaking, he readjusts his hands so that he's not keeping me pressed against his face, his tongue an assault on my over-sensitized pussy. Gripping me again, never once jabbing me with his shadow claws, he hefts me up in the air before drop-ping me down on my feet.

I'm wobbly. Unsteady. Dizzy, too, when the monster spins me quickly.

Next thing I know, my hands are braced against the closet's door frame. Determined, he positions me so my back is arched, ass out.

Fast as a flash, I feel something nudging against the entrance to my tender pussy. I'm so wet, he slides right through my folds, and his grunt of frustration that he couldn't just shove himself inside of me makes me realize what the hell is going on.

It was one thing to let him go down on me. I was too stunned that he was real to even think about stopping him, and it felt so amazing, I didn't *want* him to stop.

This is something different. I let this big monster seduce me last night because I thought he wasn't real. That it was just another one in a long line of sex dreams starring an impossible demon.

But he *is* real. And until I can figure out how that happened, and why I dreamed of him before some book I've been obsessed with brought him to life, I'm not about to fuck him again.

I don't bother trying to explain. More details from last night are coming back to me—including the fact that he didn't speak a lick of English or seem to react at all to anything I said.

Besides, if my hunch is right, I don't have to explain. I just have to go where the shadow monster can't reach me.

Before he can get a second chance to stick his dick in me, I drop low, snagging one of the dresses that knocked to the floor while I was writhing against the closet rack. Then, hoping like hell this works, I skip across the room.

I park myself into the brightest patch of sunlight that there is before quickly yanking the dress on over my head.

I'm not sure why, but something tells me that it's not a good idea to be naked around this inexplicably irresistible monster.

LOKI

I want nothing more than to taste my female again, but when she shakes her head, gesturing for me to stay in the shadows as she skips out into the light, I know that I must wait.

I find the prospect of it easier with our mate bond in place. From the moment her dark yet strangely dim eyes looked right into mine, the bond snapping as I instantly recognized that this human female is mine, I know that there is nothing I won't do to please her.

Even if she won't let me pleasure her.

I do not understand why she's putting distance between us. She must know that I am her male. Why else would she welcome me so readily? My mating instincts spurred me to claim her immediately while also acknowledging our bond. She was just as eager, mewling to me in her human words, moaning in a language so universal, I lost my seed almost immediately after I worked my cock inside of her heat.

She knew she was mine last night. She cleaved to me, in both my demon form and when I was my shadows. I allowed both halves of myself to learn my wee human female, adoring the way her cool touch shocked my skin.

Because she touched me. Intimately and possessively, my mate touched me all over. She was obviously trying to give me her essence, though she did not speak the mate's promise. At least, she did not in Sombran, though I can't say for sure she wasn't promising me everything in her human language.

Without an essence exchange, I cannot tell.

She tried to give me hers while I searched for a drop to share with her. Splayed out beneath me, her cunt full of all the seed I gave her, I had no essence at all for my mate. That's the downside of being demonic, and why so many of my kind fear losing themselves to the shadows. No essence means no mate's promise.

But it doesn't mean no bond. I cling to that myself as my human mate chatters to herself in her language, hurriedly pulling on a covering that keeps me from watching her breasts bob and scenting my musk on her oddly pale skin.

Almost as white as the duke of Sombra's, my mate's flesh is as pale as her eyes are dark. Her hair is a softer shade, not as shadowy as mine, and almost as long. Once she has her coverings on—my chest rumbles when I see she's wearing a human dress, leaving me free to reach beneath the skirt for her cunt when she's ready to welcome me again—she picks up her hair, tossing it behind her shoulders.

Her breasts jut forward. Even with the fabric covering on, I see the outline of them. My fingers itch to touch them again. They were softer than ungez fur and fit perfectly in my hand.

I wonder how they would taste. Comparable to her cunt? As a student before I went fully demonic, I did research at the School of Mages. Perhaps now it is time to study my mate again.

The light from the human world will weaken me, but it is worth it to approach my female.

When the sunlight sizzled against my shadow form earlier, I realized that my time at the edge of Sombra had me accustomed to the darkness. I thought about melting into the shadows beneath her bed but then I wouldn't have been able to see her slumber. Through the slight crack between the door to the small den and the rest of her sleeping quarters, I could watch her from these shadows.

I no longer want to just watch her. I *need* to touch her again.

I inch my bare foot out of the small den she has in her quarters.

She throws her hands up. "Hangone derebuddee. Watar udoon? Nonono."

Ah. The rest of her language is gibberish, but I think I understand the 'no' sound. She doesn't want me to leave the shadows.

She must worry about the light weakening me. And while it shall, even then I am strong enough to protect her from anyone who might threaten her.

"Mate," I say, my voice coming out deeper thanks to the need rushing through me. "Fear not." I tip my head, making sure she can see both sets of my horns. "Your male is a two-horn."

She squeals. It's a high-pitched sound and I puff out my chest. Obviously, she is quite pleased to see that I am one of the powerful demons who has two sets of horns instead of only one.

To show her that I understand, I reach up, stroking the horn in front.

She clutches her breast.

I grin. She is impressed by her male and, though I cannot tell her with words that I would love to lay my palm on one of her mounds, she is offering it to me.

Another step closer. The light makes my shadows faint. With the promise of getting to mate my female again, I shift from my nearly transparent form to my solid shape. I'd prefer to be shadow while I took her again—the sensation was *incredible*—but the light is too strong for me to hold that shape. Taking her as a demon will have to work for now.

I must have made a good concession because her dark eyes immediately drop to my hard cock.

When I'm in my shadows, my features aren't as notable as they are when I'm solid. That's on purpose. In a realm like Sombra, it's a camouflage against the dangers in our world. Our bright eyes illuminate the outline of our horns, our nose, and the protective ridges near our brow. Lower, certain details are hidden unless I'm right in front of you.

Solid, with my bare feet flat against her smooth floor, she can see every inch of me. No surprise that she seems entranced by my cock.

It is quite impressive, I must say. I only have one—unlike the demons in Mellizos, a realm where the males have *two* similar to my double set of horns—but it certainly was enough to pleasure my mate in the time of the shadows.

Even larger when I'm solid, I know she can take me. She did before, and I'd walk through fire to get her to do so again.

"My mate." I crook my claw at her. "Come to your male."

"Ohnoe. Imnut fawlin ferdat gen."

Yes, my mate. I know I am large and you are wee. But the gods granted you as my mate and you are perfect for me.

"Come to Loki," I tell her, my voice as cajoling as I can make it.

When she starts to move, I believe that she finally

understood what I asked. She does not. Instead of walking toward me, she tiptoes away before breaking across the room. I watch her curiously. I've heard of bonded couples who prefer to play a game before mating. The female runs, the male chases, and when he catches his female, he takes her where he finds her.

There isn't much room for my human mate to run from me. Even if I wasn't a master tracker and hunter, she only goes to the other side of her quarters.

Is this her way of making the hunt easy for her male? If it is, I wish I could tell her that she need not bother. She might not be the demoness I imagined would be mine, but she is beautiful to me. She does not need to trigger my mating instincts to get me to mount her.

From the moment she woke from her slumber and our eyes met, bond snapping into place, my cock has not gone down yet. I will always be prepared to mate her.

As I start toward her, she squeals again. She says something else in her human language, too quick for me to even try to understand, before she reaches for a thick book she has on the furniture near her bed.

I freeze when I recognize it, even from across her quarters.

Where did she get that?

It looks like it belongs in the archives of Marvo. I should know. The scroll with the matefinder spell had been marked with a sigil such as that.

Is this how she found me? Using her human magic to summon me with an age-old spell? It would explain how I was able to resist the initial call. My magic is long gone, but I *am* still a mage deep down.

And my amazing human mate is a witch in her own right if she can cast spells from a Sombran grimoire.

Seeing the book slaps me right out of my mating haze. I do not know how my mate got her tiny little hands on that book, but it reminds me that I once stole from Duke Haures. I was banished, then left to suffer in the shadows for my crime.

What if he discovers that I found my mate in a human and, instead of immediately leaving the human realm after I claimed her, I lingered because I could not bring myself to leave her bed until it was too late?

The ruler of Sombra can be forgiving when it comes to mate bonds, but I can not break the first law. To do so would be to earn a pair of enchanted chains and a stay in his dungeon. Add that to being a thief and I might be sentenced to execution.

To die after finally finding my mate? After how long I waited for her, and all I survived in the shadows?

I could not risk it.

Besides, this female is *mine*. She was born for me, meant for me, and she summoned me to her. The gods have given me this glorious beauty, and I will accept their bounty gratefully.

Of course she will be happy and join me in Sombra. It is where I can protect her and keep her close. Provide for her and pleasure her. Love her and worship her. There I will work hard to find some essence, to earn her mate's promise, and give her forever.

In Sombra, my mortal will become *immortal* and I will have forever to learn about this female.

Starting with what exactly she means when she squeals again and says, "Gottabbe sum waytoo git riduvim."

Is she professing her love to me already? I choose to think so, even as the slightest hint of nerves begins to wind its way into her sweet scent. I understand. Demons are raised with their instincts guiding them to find their forever mate. Maybe it's not the same for humans. Maybe she is worried that I won't love her so soon.

She would be mistaken. I've loved her from the moment our eyes met, and I'll love her still with every breath.

We only just met, but she is the reason my heart beats. And if it pleased her, I would give it to her now.

But since I can't find the words to tell her so, I decide it is time we go home. Once I don't have to worry about risking the duke's wrath, I can start working toward showing my mate how no male will love her better than I.

Her funny little nose is buried in the pages of the spellbook. Flipping the pages frantically, as though she's searching for a spell to re-open the portal that summoned me here from Sombra, I decide to do it for her.

She is full of magic. One of us should be. She can save her stores while I use my demon nature to bring us home. Now that we're bonded, I can handle this part.

First, though, I need to gather her close. I doubt she is familiar with travel between planes—Duke Haures isn't the only demon ruler who has cut off our world from the mortal realm—and I do not want her to be frightened.

She's still reading as I return to my shadow form, winking out and reappearing in the patch of black hovering in the corner of her quarters. I surprise myself at how easy that was. It seems as if, even in the human realm, a Sombra demon has control over the shadows.

"Hold on tight, my mate," I tell her, gripping her by her waist and turning her into me.

"Watha—" Her head whips up. She has the same creased look on her adorable face as she did earlier when I hoisted her up and buried my face against her cunt.

"I wish I could," I tell her honestly. Of course. I

can never lie to my mate. "But mating will have to wait until we are back in Sombra."

"Sombra," she squeaks. "Didjusay *Sombra*? Lyk mi buk?"

I'm not sure what she means, but I nod because she echoes 'Sombra'. She must be asking if we are leaving now.

And then, with one quick heft, I lift her so that she is tossed over my shoulder. Portal travel is safe, but I do not trust the shadows of Sombra. Any threat could be waiting for our arrival and I need at least one set of claws free.

"Lemmeego." She slaps at my shadows. "Lemmeego!"

"I won't drop you. You have my word. Now hold still, my mate. We'll be in Sombra in a moment."

Creating a portal back to Sombra is instinctive for a bonded demon. With my mate tucked securely over my shoulder, I simply want to return to the shadows and a pathway opens in front of me.

I leap right through it, landing in a crouch on the other side of the portal.

Thank the gods that the portal brought us right into my shack. I had worried that we would arrive in the shadows or, even worse, the village I abandoned ages ago. With my mate traveling with me, I don't know what would have been worse: being confronted by other demons who might try to steal her from me, or the beasts in the dark who might try to hurt her.

Rising up, I shift her slight weight, setting her on the floor.

"Here we are, my mate. It is our home."

She's clutching the book to her chest. It made it through the portal with her, and she's squeezing it so tightly, I can sense the edge cutting into her arm through our mate bond. Without her essence, I don't know what she's thinking. Is she pleased with my home? Is she ready to mate again? What about food. Should I feed her?

I should feed her.

"Are you hungry, my mate? What do humans eat? I shall feed you."

She's not listening to me. Spinning on her heel, eyes wide, she's looking around my quarters, taking it all in.

I wait with bated breath.

And that's when my mate begins to scream.

CHAPTER 6
WHERE AM I

KENNEDY

It all happens so fast.

That's a cliché, right? When you're caught up in a moment and something happens that you can't stop, it seems like it all goes down in the blink of an eye, but it doesn't *really*.

What just happened? No. That did.

Mainly because I had no idea how fast the monster could move.

A few moments ago, he was standing on the edge of my closet. When he flashed his high beams at me, I was instantly thrown back to last night. Add in the way his lips curved around his fangs, claw crooked at me as he murmured in his deep voice, and I knew he was thinking about what happened, too.

The massive hard-on he was sporting was another big clue.

Because he was hiding in the shadows when I woke up—and he was obviously *real*—I quickly changed my mind. I didn't fuck an incubus in my dreams, but lucky me, I'm pretty sure I got lucky with the bogeyman. I think he's the monster who hides in closets, but he wasn't waiting to scare me. Or to eat me.

Oh, no, I think. He was waiting to eat me out.

After I disentangled myself from him, snagging the dress that fell on the floor before I stumbled on shaking legs out into the morning sunlight, I thought I got away from him. Not like I was scared or anything. Despite him being some kind of monster, fear was the last thing I felt, though I was quickly getting over my horniness when I thought of *his* horns.

He has *four* of them. That seems like four too many in the daylight now.

What kind of monster even *has* four?

I don't know. And when he kept looking at me like he was already imagining shoving that massive dick inside of me again, I did what I always do: I turn to a book.

I figured it was safe. He wouldn't risk the sunlight, and I could take a few seconds to grab the *Grimoire du Sombra* and see if I missed the big honking passage that said my 'true love' was going to be a big shadow monster who made me come harder than I ever had before.

Because the spell worked. Obviously. It might not have worked straight away, but I can't come up with any other explanation for how the big demon-looking guy found his way into my room *and* I thought it was a good idea to let him seduce me.

I can blame it on being a dream all I want. I know better. I might get a pass for last night. This morning? I'm wide awake, and I'm freaking out a bit.

Thinking I was untouchable on the other side of my sunny room, I frantically flipped through the spell-book. He was talking to me, the words gruff and harsh. His monster language, I figure, and none of it makes sense to me. He keeps repeating one phrase over and over again—*uxor mi*, or something like that—and the way he absently trails his hand along his dick makes me wonder what *that* could be monster-speak for.

His tone is cajoling. Even if I can't translate his words, I know exactly what he wants.

Me.

Not happening, buddy.

So, yeah. One second he was hanging out in my closet. It was probably my fault for thinking he would stay there. For a few seconds, I take my eyes off of him.

A few seconds is all he needs.

I don't even see him move. He's there, then he's

not. He's in the closet, then he's looming behind me, laying his hands on my waist. A gasp escapes me as he whirls me around.

"What the—"

He's saying something. The heat of his palms is distracting me at the same time as I wonder how in the hell did he get behind me without me seeing. As he speaks, only one word sticks out to me.

Sombra.

"Sombra? Did you just say 'Sombra'? Like my book?"

He nods. I get the feeling that he only does so because I expect him to, not because he has any clue what I just asked him—especially since he follows that by lifting me high, tossing me over his shoulder.

"Let me go," I shout, hitting the bulk of his back. He's a mass of shadows, my fingers dipping past the unformed edges of him. I still find something to hit and, big as he is, I put a little effort into it. "Let me go!"

It doesn't work.

Before I can try some other way to catch his attention, a rush of heat slams into me. It's coming from my right side. Jerking my head, I'm stunned speechless when I see a… honestly, I don't know what to call it. Hole, maybe? It's a big, swirling black hole stretching from the floor to about a foot higher than the monster's horns. The heat's coming from in there, and when he turns, loping toward it, I almost swallow my tongue in my hurry to shout again.

He leaps, and the black void swallows my scream.

The fall forward is over as soon as it begins. He lands in a graceful crouch, popping up quickly before patting my ass and setting me down on my feet.

The first thing I notice is that it's not as hot as it was; it's actually cooler than my room had been. The floor is solid yet dusty beneath my bare feet. It has a distinctly sulfurous stink—like rotten eggs—that has me choking as I stumble away from him.

He shadows my every move, watching me closely.

Glancing away from the monster, my eyes sweep across the room. It's dark in here. Not because there's no light. There is. A gentle white floating light is posted in each corner of the room, hovering over an iron sconce. A candle? Maybe. It's weird, but as I blink my eyes, getting used to the small amount of illumination, I see that it's so dark in here because the walls are a dingy black.

A shiny break on one wall is possibly a window. I don't see a door, though I do spy a bed that's big enough for a monster his size to sleep in without his feet hanging over the edge. At least, I *think* it's a bed. It's more like a collapsed dome with a dip in the center, an inky black sheet following its strange shape, making it look more like a nest.

There's only one other thing in this room besides

the weird nest, the hovering monster, the book I'm still clutching tightly to my chest, and me.

Hanging on the dark wall, propped up on some type of shelf, is a… a…

Oh my God.

It's a skull.

It's a *human* skull.

Why does this monster have a human skull hanging up in the corner of his room like some kind of trophy?

Yeah… that's when I scream again.

His pointed ears twitch. We don't need to be able to understand each other to know that a scream is universal in any language. He hears my scream and immediately lowers himself into a crouch again.

Making himself smaller, I think. He knows I'm frightened. I get the feeling that he doesn't want me to be.

When he reaches his hand for me, I jump a few steps back. If he touches me, I'll let him. So that I can convince myself that maybe this *is* a dream, that he didn't actually steal me right out of my bedroom, I'd let him.

I can't let him.

What else can I do?

The window, I think. Spinning away from him, my skirt whirling around my knees, I dart for the window.

I don't know why it seems so important for me to

look outside of it. It's already obvious he brought me somewhere. Picked me up like a sack of potatoes and jumped into a swirling black void in the middle of my room and now we're here.

Only one problem: where is *here*?

The window doesn't help. It's a thicker type of glass than I've ever seen before, with no way to open it. At first, I'm almost sure it's been blacked out. That's how dark it is outside. I see nothing except shadows upon shadows until a pair of glowing eyes appear in the distance.

White, just like the monster's. They're low on the ground, so I don't think it's another one of him, but they belong to some*thing*. Something just like him, and nothing like I've ever seen back in New York.

Back on *Earth*.

A knot forms in my stomach as I finally land on the easy conclusion:

I'm not on Earth anymore, am I?

My throat is raw from my scream, my voice notably shaky as I demand, "Where am I? Where did you take me?"

"Uxor mi—"

Nope. Not that again.

"Take me back," I tell him. Doesn't matter that I know he doesn't understand English. I try anyway. I wave my arm in a circle, miming the portal that brought us here. "Bring me home."

Between my gesture and my tone, it should be

easy for him to figure out what I want. However, before he has to come up with a way to refuse— because, believe me, I know that's coming—the most awkward thing happens.

My stomach grumbles loud enough that we both hear it.

His forehead creases. He works his jaw, like he's trying to figure out what to say but can't come up with the words. As panic crests over me, my breath coming short and fast, he stands the rest of the way up.

Holy hell, he's big. Was he this big back in Jericho? Was he this big when I let him push that monster dick inside of me?

Considering how tender and achy I'm feeling, yes. Yes, he was.

With a firm look on his shadowed face, he gestures for me to stay where I am.

Right, I think a touch hysterically. Because where else am I going to go?

———

I MISSED A DOOR ON MY EARLIER INSPECTION. THE seam is so close to the wall that it's hidden where the light doesn't reach. Until he pushes against it and it swings outward into another room, I thought he was going to float right through the wall.

Can he do that? I wouldn't be surprised if he could.

Moving closer to one of the lights, I do a double-take when I realize that it wasn't just giving the illusion of floating over the sconce. It *is* floating, like magic.

Okay, then.

I couldn't care less how it does it. Letting the spellbook fall open into my arms, I take the moment without the shadow monster to go back to flipping through the pages, looking for some way to reverse whatever it is that I did.

Last night, I only paid attention to the page Shannon had marked with her receipt. When nothing happened, I closed it and immediately forgot about it for the first time since I sold her the damn thing.

The rest of the pages have the same typeface. Other spells, I figure, or something else. I can't tell. It's all in the same strange language—the same one the horned monster speaks, I'm betting—and whoever marked up the 'true love' spell wasn't decent enough to translate anything else.

I go back to the page marked **VERUS AMOR**, a trembling finger traveling down the print until I reach the second big paragraph.

Promise, I think. I know what 'manifest' means now, but what about 'promise'?

It isn't worth the risk. With my luck, I could read the second passage and somehow promise to be his sex slave for all eternity or something.

No, thanks.

I'm still leafing through the book when the door swings open again. Striding purposely back into the room where he left me is the same monster from before.

He's still the shadow man version who first joined me in my bed before he went solid. Even so, it's getting easier for me to pick out his features in the darkness. His fangs peeking past his bottom lips help, a gleaming white almost as striking against his black form as his strange eyes.

He holds out his arm. Something is dangling from his grip. It's made up of the same shadows as my monster, though it's much smaller. As he moves closer to me, the light helps me see exactly what it is.

It's so not what I was expecting.

The shadows are fluffier than the monster's. Giving the impression of a fuzzy fur, he's holding a creature that has a cat's pointed face and triangle-shaped ears, a pair of rodent teeth, white eyes like the monster's, and a tail the same length and curve as a squirrel's.

It's hanging from the monster's dark hand, chittering softly.

He holds it out, expecting me to take it from him.

I back up.

He shoves it at me again. "Ungez." With his other hand, he reaches up to his mouth, gesturing at his fangs as he pretends to bite the air. "Cachin."

I get it now. My stomach grumbled, and he went

out to… what? Hunt me some meat, I figure. Only he brought back something that isn't only alive, it reminds me of a cross between a cat and a squirrel.

The creature chatters, twisting its body like a coil, looking at the beast, then me, then at the beast.

And then it starts to *purr*.

How can he expect me to eat something that adorable?

Maybe the monsters do. Big shadow demon beast, tiny little shadow animal, it's the way of the food chain, I guess.

Not me, especially when he places the critter—the *ungez*, I'm thinking—near my feet, nudging it closer to me with one of his. Immediately, the squirrel-cat hops up, shadowy claws hooking on my skirt before it scurries up my chest, launching onto my shoulder, wrapping its tail around the back of my neck.

It purrs even louder, and I decide then and there that I'd rather starve than eat this little guy.

I lift my fingers, only a little nervous it might be vicious after all. When all it does is nuzzle closer to me, I run my fingers through its shadows. Whether it's a trick of my senses or it really is that soft, I sense fur.

The monster's frowning when I glance over at him. He doesn't look offended that I'm petting my meal instead of chowing down. And when he reaches for it and I throw up a hand, preventing him from taking it from me, his eyes dim, like he's thinking it over.

Then, for the second time, he gestures for me to stay where I am.

So long as I can keep the shadow critter, sure.

At least until I can figure out a way to go back home, that is.

CHAPTER 7
UN UNGEZ

KENNEDY

He's gone longer this time. While he's missing, I plop down on the bed… nest… *whatever* because it was either that or the dusty floor. The squirrel-cat travels down my arm once I do, nestling in my lap.

As if I hadn't already decided to keep it for now.

Stroking its fur, comforted by its gentle purr, I force myself to come to grips with my situation. I have to. Something tells me that I'm going to be sticking around for a bit. The book was no help, and until I can get the monster to understand that he has to bring me back, I don't think he's just going to offer.

Not until he gets what he wants. And if he does? I'll never get to leave.

I've gone through all the emotions. Fear. Anger. Anxiety. Determination.

Kennedy adapts. Kennedy survives.

If a big monster wants to take her on, he can try. But she will always, always come out on top.

After last night and this morning, he wants me. I want to go home. Let's see who gets what they want first.

With a new game plan in mind, I'm much calmer by the time he finally returns. I do regret that I didn't grab my phone off the charger before I went to my closet this morning. Not because I expected my service plan to extend to another world, but because I didn't realize how much I'd grown used to it telling me the time until I can't.

He could've been gone twenty minutes. It could've been an hour. Maybe three. I don't know. In the quiet of the room, with only the squirrel-cat's purr breaking up the eerie silence, I wish I'd grabbed my phone. My Kindle. *Anything*.

Oh, yeah. I need to go home. For my store. For my *sanity*. I can't stay here—

—and then the door opens and, when I see him, my heart skips a beat. The strange unsettling feeling I'd had while he was gone disappears as soon as I meet his triumphant gaze. Like I feel better just having him near.

What the *hell*?

Distraction, I think. I need a distraction, and boy

do I get one when I get a better look at the monster and see that he came back with one of the squirrel-cats squirming in each of his hands.

Oh, no. Oh, he *didn't*.

See? This is what a language barrier gets you. I saved one squirrel-cat from being a meal, and what did he do? Go out and get me *two* more.

He looks so pleased, too. Like he found the secret to my happiness and it's him bringing me these strange shadows animals no matter why I might want them.

I'm pretty sure he doesn't get the concept of pets. If he does, he probably doesn't think these creatures qualify since he already tried to feed me one. And yet… he brought me more.

I don't want more. I probably shouldn't keep the first one. I have no idea what they eat or what they are or if, like him, the creature has a shadow form and a solid form. What if it can change shapes as easily and looks like a gremlin instead of a cute squirrel-cat?

Call me a soft touch if you will, but I feel a kinship with the first critter. Plucked by this big shadow monster, brought to his home whether we wanted to go or not… and it still looks pretty damn happy to be snuggled up on his bed.

And where am I right now? The same spot.

Moving the first squirrel-cat to the edge of the dip in the nest, I hop up, waving my hands at him.

He preens, showing off the squirming creatures.

"Just one," I tell him, holding up my pointer finger. "I just want one."

"Un?"

'Un' sounds enough like 'uno' for me. "Yes! Just one."

"Un ungez?"

That's the squirrel-cat. "Yes. Un ungez."

He nods once, then turns around still swinging the creatures by their tails. I remember too late that he initially brought me the creature to eat and I hope he's not going to snack on them in front of me.

To my surprise, he doesn't. Walking past me, he shifts his hold on the squirrel-cats until he has both of them in one hand. He does something in front of the window. Turns out it opens after all because it's suddenly a hole in the wall, allowing him to drop the creatures back outside before the window closes on its own.

That done, he starts gesturing for me to stay put again.

This time I stop him.

I have to. Part of me wonders if he's going to decide I need more of these shadow pets after all, while the other half is terrified to find out what he's going to bring me next.

He seems to be trying to please me. Of course. It doesn't take a genius to figure out why he decided to take me home with him. If this is some sort of beastly bachelor pad, then I'm guessing the monster who seduced me last night was looking for a Mrs. and I seemed to fit the bill.

The language barrier is too big to overcome right now. I have to admit that. But while I now know that my new pet is an *ungez*, I have no idea what my sensual lover turned captor is.

I don't even know his *name*.

I have his complete attention. He stays still on his side of the room, watching me closely.

I tap my chest.

His eyes light up when I manage to jab myself right in the boob. He hurries forward, reaching one of his mitt-sized hands out, ready to get a handful of tit himself next.

Uh-uh. Letting him touch me is what got me into this mess in the first place.

I hold up my hand. "No."

He immediately stops. Cocking his head to the side, his hair spilling in front of his chest, he mimics the sound. "No?"

Oh, boy. How did I forget how gruff and deep and *sexy* his voice can be? Just because I didn't understand anything he said to me while we were fucking doesn't mean that it didn't do something to hear him. It's like his voice was made for dirty talk, though he could've been saying anything at all when he kept calling me "uxor" over and over again before.

But, just like back in the apartment, it seems as if some words and gestures are universal. I say 'no' and he immediately drops his outstretched hand back to his side.

Of course, my gaze follows it as he does—and that just means I get another eyeful of his bobbing erection.

I gulp. Looking at it beneath the strange white light has me wondering not for the first time how the hell something that size ever fit inside of me. It's a good thing I'd been convinced he was some kind of dream because if I knew then that he was real… I would've been afraid of being split apart by his dick. Now I know I won't be— not that I plan on trying him on for size again.

Right?

Giving my head a clearing shake, I force my gaze back to his face.

Okay. Let's try this again.

I tap my chest. "Kennedy. My name is Kennedy."

He frowns.

Okay. Probably too much for a first lesson. "Kennedy." I circle my finger around my face. "Kennedy."

"Ah," he says. He jabs a claw in my direction. "Ken-dee."

Hey. Close enough.

"Yes," I say, nodding so he puts the syllable to the action. I point at myself. "Kennedy."

"Ken-dee."

I point at him and wait.

"Loki," he grates out.

Did I—

I point at me again.

"Ken-dee."

I point at him.

"Loki."

—I *did.*

I almost laugh as I realize the shadow monster's name. Only the look of pride on his monstrous features as he repeats it one more time for good measure keeps me from giggling. He says it in two distinct syllables—"low key"—but I'm one hundred percent sure that my demon shares the same name as the Norse trickster god—and the gorgeous villain in the Thor movies.

I clear my throat so that he doesn't realize I think his name is amusing. At least we're getting somewhere. I can stop thinking of him as a "monster" and a "beast', and he can—

"Ken-dee," he repeats, pointing at me. He turns his claws toward his bare chest. "Loki."

And then he gestures at his erection.

Okay, then. I'm going to have to remember that, despite us not being able to communicate, he isn't stupid. Using the few words we both know—our names—I'm pretty sure he just used use some old-fashioned ingenuity to try to initiate sex again.

I'll give him points for effort and determination.

Doesn't mean that I'm going to christen that bed with him.

So I pretend not to understand. "What?"

He widens his stance, as though he thinks my feigned confusion is because I don't see the big dick jutting out from his hairless groin. Then, just in case, he wiggles his hips, showing it off.

Yeah… I should've known better. And it's not like I haven't been inexplicably attracted to him since he appeared in my room. Compared to him, I must look tiny and pale and strange, but that doesn't seem to bother him. Just like his alien features should scare me instead of turning me on.

I shake my head. Last night was a mistake since it obviously gave him the wrong idea.

Another frown. "Uxor mi—"

There's that 'uxor' again.

I'm pretty sure I know what *that* means now.

But I can't. No matter how good it was, I can't fuck him again. That would only tell him that he made the right choice, tossing me over his shoulder and bringing me to his world. I'm a (somewhat) strong, (kind of) independent businesswoman. I'm not going to let him control me with sex.

Especially since I only just learned his name.

So, slashing my hand across the air, I say in as determined a voice as I can muster, "Uxor *no*."

No sex. Once I can excuse as me being out of my mind when the book I obsessed over for a week brought a hulking monster right into my bedroom. The oral he gave me was amazing, but a part of me was still convinced I was dreaming when he lifted me up onto his shoulders.

I'm not dreaming now, though I almost wish I was when Loki picks up on what I'm saying.

His eyes flare. Brighter than an industrial flashlight, they gleam out of his face. It's hard to tell with the light basically blinding me, but I'm pretty sure he looks angry.

Good going, Kennedy. Why not piss off the beastly demon who kidnapped you after you said 'hello' by impaling yourself onto his dick instead of shaking his hand?

First his eyes flared, but now it's his nostrils turn. Breathing in deep, he turns off the high beams.

His gruff voice takes on the familiar cajoling sound I remember vividly from last night. "Kendee..."

Uh-uh. He's not seducing me again. Especially since there's a part of me that almost wants to *let* him.

"I mean it," I tell him, not caring that he has no clue what I'm saying. It makes me feel better, and now that his flash of anger disappeared as quickly as it came, my voice gets stronger. "No more sex. I don't know who you are or what you want with me" —well, except for what he already got last night— "but I'm pretty sure sex is just going to complicate things."

I'm babbling. Can't help it. It's like I feel the need to explain.

Just like he needs to give it one more try.

He waves at his dick, then gestures at me.

I shake my head.

He could force me. No matter what happened last night and how I try to justify it as believing it was a dream, I was a willing participant in everything that we did. I fucked a huge shadow monster, and if he really pushed it, I would do it again.

I don't have to.

Shrugging, he finally takes his big dick in hand. Then, shifting his body so that I can watch if I want, he begins to stroke it.

He starts off slow. A few leisurely strokes to get into a rhythm before his fist becomes a shadowy blur, covering his cock from root to tip before I can sense the motion of his hand.

He treats it like a task. There is no seduction here. No teasing glance my way, no third invitation to have sex with him. He works his cock like he has a checklist that he's trying to complete.

Seduce human woman.

Kidnap her and keep her in the bedroom.

Feed her a squirrel-cat.

Bring her two more when she expresses an interest in keeping it.

Get off.

Since I'm not willing, he takes what he can get: his hand.

Me? I get a show.

I watch as the muscles in his big body move. In barely no time, his back goes taut, legs planted firmly on the floor. Eyes meeting mine, he fists his fingers around the head of his cock, catching his jizz from spraying all over the floor.

He doesn't blink the entire time he's coming, only looking away when he's done.

And none of that should have been as hot as it was.

I MAY HAVE BEEN ABLE TO GET LOKI TO UNDERSTAND that I have no intention of fucking him again. After he rubbed one out, he acted as though he wasn't walking around stark naked with an erection that could poke an eye out.

Fine with me.

When it comes to his sudden fixation with feeding me?

Yeah. That one's a lost cause.

After he gets his release, he disappears from the room again. I have to work hard to keep my fingers to myself. I might have been well and truly pleasured recently by him, but that just made me realize what I was missing out on since I left Tyler's cheating ass.

I want more pleasure, and it would be a mistake to have it right now.

I can't even take care of my own need. How much do you want to bet that Loki would take me touching myself on his bed as an open invitation if he walked in on me with my fingers on my pussy?

I'm already in big, big trouble. I don't want it to get any worse.

My new pet is an amazing distraction. Since I can't pay attention to one pussy, I give all the rest of it to the chittering, friendly little squirrel-cat.

I decide to name it… well *her* since I also decide she's a *she*… I name her Freya after the Norse goddess who traveled in a chariot pulled by cats. Considering my beastly captor is Loki, that's the direction my thoughts went in and I ran with it.

She's definitely more cat. Growing up, my family always had at least one living with us so I consider myself a bit of an expert. The way Freya curls on her back, batting her paws as I poke them gently reminds me of a kitten. She also has this fascination with curling up around my neck which I appreciate that's very cat-like.

It's growing colder out. The slight chill from earlier has become much cooler the longer I'm stuck in here. All I have is the sundress I tugged on over my head and a makeshift scarf courtesy of Freya's fluffy, shadow tail, and that's not really enough.

I'm pretty hungry, too. I couldn't bring myself to

eat my new pet, but I need something. The last thing I had was a bowl of cereal before I went to bed last night and who knows how long ago that was?

Once again he proves that he's much more intuitive and adaptive than I would have thought. When Loki returns again, his hands are full. No *ungez*, though, which is a relief until I realize what he is holding.

It's a hunk of raw meat, stripped from the bone.

On the plus side, it's a bigger chunk than you'd get from an animal as small as Freya. I don't think he skinned one of the *ungez* to feed me.

But he certainly skinned something.

Just in case, I gesture at the raw meat, then point at Freya.

His horns dip, brow furrowing. He thinks about what I could mean for a moment before he straightens again.

"Ungez," Loki grunts, pointing at my pet with his claws. Hefting the raw meat up in his palm, he says, "Jabila."

I have to believe that means it's not the same. And I'm sure, if he brought me the meat without butchering it first, I'd have a hard time eating it. But he's learning how to keep Kennedy a lot quicker than I would've thought.

Only one problem. I'm hungry. I'll admit that. Fry me up a steak and I'll eat it. If I convince myself that's what *jabila* means in his language, I can at least try what he has.

There's no way I can choke it down like that.

"Aren't you going to cook it?" I ask him. "Cook. Loki cook?"

"Ken-dee?"

He doesn't get it. Crap. How do I mime 'cook' in a way that he'll understand?

Does he even know what fire is? Considering how cold this room is, I'm not so sure.

I gotta try.

"Cook," I repeat. I hold up my hands like I'm pretending to warm them in front of a fire. "Cook. Fire." I mime it again before pointing to the meat, then my mouth. "Cook and Kennedy eat."

He regards the hunk of meat thoughtfully and holds it up in one hand.

Loki folds his other fist tight. When he releases it, there's a small ball of *fire* hovering over his palm.

I squeal, excited that he figured out what I meant and also stunned that the shadow monster can create fire in his hand.

I'm not the only one, either.

Loki looks as surprised as I am.

CHAPTER 8
WATER AND FIRE

KENNEDY

The way I see it, if I'm going to be here for a while—and I can't see how I'm going home anytime soon—I'm going to make the most of it.

Starting with taking care of my new pet.

After she nibbled on a few pieces of meat I offered her, she hopped up on the bed, making herself a little nest near the top. She seems right at home here.

Lucky Freya.

I ate as much of the cooked meat as I could manage before Loki's intense expression made me too uncomfortable. Crouching in front of the bed where I found my seat, I don't see his bobbing cock even though I know it's there. We've come to an unspoken agreement not to pay any attention to it, as though he's trying to prove he's not only keeping me for sex.

He fed me. Just when I'm wondering how I'm going to wash my hands—or, for God's sake, *pee*—he grunts and jerks his head toward the door. Moving over to it, he rumbles his version of my name.

"Ken-dee."

Since he wants to lead me out of the obvious bedroom, I decide to follow. I'm glad I did. Loki brings me into the second room. It's as empty as the bedroom—no skulls in here, I notice—but I see two strange structures along one wall.

One is a narrow black tube about four inches wide. It comes up from the ground, hitting Loki at his navel. That means, for me, it's as tall as my boobs. Next to it is a crystalline cup that twinkles beneath the same floating lights he has in his bedroom.

I understand why when he waves his massive hand over the tube and, to my surprise—and delight—a stream of water arcs out of the tube and into a square-shaped hole built into the floor.

It's rimmed with the same dark metal as the tube so I know the hole's there on purpose. Peeking into it, it's so black, it looks bottomless.

After dipping his glass under the stream of water, he takes a sip, then offers it to me. I don't even hesitate. I've never been so thirsty before.

I prepare myself for it to be lukewarm and muddy. It's not. To be fair, the water is cool and crisp and really, really good. It tastes *clean*. Refreshing. As he watches me gulp it down, all I can think about is having more.

Once it's empty, I hand it back to him. He doesn't even ask. Waving his hand over the tube again, he refills the cup. The stream ends as soon as he moves the cup away, handing it back to me.

I sip it more leisurely this time. It tastes just as good as it did when I downed it, but I stop once I've quenched my thirst.

I have to. I haven't peed yet since I woke up and I'd rather not have to figure out a way to tell Loki that I have to.

Turns out, I don't.

Making sure he has my attention, Loki pours the last of the water into the hole. Seems like a bit of a waste to me until he uses one claw to point at the cup, then waves his hand at his cock.

My cheeks heat up as he draws my attention back to it. I know that wasn't what he meant—when he scoots closer to the hole, bracing his legs like human guys do at the urinal, I figure I'm looking at his version of a toilet—but I can't help it.

I should be grateful there's some fresh water and somewhere to pee. It might have been a worry at the back of my mind when I realized I wasn't in the human world anymore, but it was there. But one small relief taken care of just means I have room to remember last night again.

Loki's head tilts, his gaze sweeping over me. This close, I see it when his nostrils flare. As animalistic as he acts, when he starts rumbling in his chest again, I realize that his nose is a lot stronger than I want it to be.

Because I'm suddenly aroused and I think he knows it.

No panties, I remember. I have on a dress and no underwear, and even though I should want to bash him over his head with that human skull he has, I feel drawn to him in a way that shouldn't make sense.

True love, whispers a little voice in my head. Annoyingly, it's in a sing-song tone. *He's your true love.*

Right.

My true love is a beast who lives in a world that makes no sense. Full of shadows and skulls and contradictions.

Take his room. It's empty. It stinks. Loki actually thought bringing me a live animal to eat was normal, and came back with raw meat before realizing I would want it cooked. I might be biased because of the language barrier and how he stole me, but he gives me straight-up caveman vibes.

But he can conjure fire in his palm. He has these strange magic lights in his rundown shelter, and a water fountain that seems motion-activated but is probably some more magic.

Not to mention it has a toilet you don't have to flush.

It's not Earth. I know that much. It's a place where magic is real and monsters take humans home with them. I'd almost be afraid that Loki thinks of me as his pet like I plan on keeping Freya if it wasn't for how much he's made it clear he wants to fuck me.

Which is why, no matter what, I can't do that again.

MY RESOLVE IS TESTED MUCH SOONER THAN I'D hoped it would be.

I don't know how long I've been here or if a day in Loki's dark world has twenty-four hours like I'm used to. It was black as night when we arrived. Watching the window, it doesn't change. It's still dark out, which might be throwing my circadian rhythm off.

Or maybe I stubbornly stay awake as long as I can because I'm avoiding having to fall asleep again, especially in his bed.

There are so many reasons why I don't want to. Least of all because of what happened last night in mine. After that charged moment when Loki masturbated in front of me, he's been careful not to mention anything about sex or *uxor*.

Message received, I guess, but for how long?

He's still naked. At first, I thought he was making a point. Like he was using the visual cue of his constant erection to remind me what we did and what he obviously wants to do again. Without him being able to guilt me that he has the monster equivalent of blue balls, I figured showing off his hard-on did the same thing.

By the time I'm struggling to keep my eyes open, I've changed my mind. I've been watching him closely. There's nothing really else for me to do, and since he can't take his eyes off of me while we're in the same room, I decide it's fair that I get to do the same.

Earlier, he stayed in his shadow form. Intangible along the edges, melting into mist when it suited him, he stayed like that whenever he left his shelter. Once he was settled in, he resumed his more demonic form: red skin, intimidating horns, white eyes, and muscles bigger than my head.

I decide that's his equivalent to taking your bra off after a long day at work. It signals that you're in for the evening. Makes sense to me. If the outside of his… house, I guess… is only shadow, he'd stand out if he didn't match.

He gives no sign that he's tired. Do monsters sleep? He has a bed, so he must, but I don't even know if he slept at all last night. I'm pretty sure I knocked out first, and then he was already awake and in my closet by the time I got up again. But the way he watches me… it's like he's afraid I'll disappear if he closes his eyes.

If I knew how to, I *would*.

Eventually, I have to admit that I can't stay up any longer. Maybe if I had my usual coffee before Loki stole me from my apartment, I might have been able to. I'm already sitting on the edge of the bed, Freya cozied up next to me; like Loki, she doesn't want to let me out of her sight. Over the next few minutes, I start to slump a little.

He catches on quick. After another round of seared meat earlier, Loki tried to join me on the bed. The moment he put his bulk down on the edge, I jumped up, Freya hopping up to follow me.

My message was clear as crystal this time. The two of us on the bed at the same time was a no-go.

Since then, he's been sitting in the shadows on the other side of the room. He doesn't hide the fact that he's staring, shifting every time I breathe wrong, but he gives me my space.

At least, he does until I finally start to curl up in the middle of the bed.

Loki immediately gets to his feet.

As tired as I am, I keep one eye quirked open. He wouldn't dare—

He does. Easing his big body over the far side of his massive bed, he's trying to join me again.

Oh, no. This monster is going to learn. Kennedy is stubborn. He wants to lay in the bed?

I'll sleep on the floor.

He huffs, patting the dip in the nest. "Ken-dee."

I shake my head. "No."

I shake my head, but as I sit cross-legged on the floor, that's not all that's got me moving.

Holy shit, it's freezing cold down here. My skirt's too short to cover anything more than my ass, and I jump back up when my bare thighs touch the ground.

Okay. I can't lay on the floor without snatching the sheet off the bed first.

That's what I was going to do—but before I can, Loki is suddenly there. I'd forgotten how fast he could be. I can barely take a step away from his solid bulk before he lays the back of his hand on my cheek.

I gasp, and then I understand.

Back at my apartment, I noticed how feverish he felt against me. His temperature was noticeably hotter than mine, but not enough to make me burn. It actually ramped up my need a little, if I'm being honest. Like Loki being hot just made me *hotter*.

I've been shivering on and off since he brought me here. The heat rushing out of the void might have been hot as hell, but his home is dark and gloomy. It feels more like late autumn/early winter in New York while I'm dressed for May.

Obviously, the chill doesn't bother Loki—I mean, he's still naked—but my fingers passed the ice cube stage a while ago.

I want a blanket. I thought about asking for one, but I'm not so sure he'd even have any. The only bedding I've seen is the surprisingly silky sheet that covers his bed. It matches the temperature in the room, too, which makes sense when the touch of his hand on my cheek feels like fire against my skin. He probably needs it to be comfortable.

And, holy shit, I need *him*.

He knows I'm cold. He knows I've been shivering, suffering silently because what else could I do?

I can use his body heat to warm me right up.

Forget my pride. Forget worrying about him taking advantage of me while I'm sleeping. That was a reach anyway since my gut tells me that my monster isn't as beastly as I've made him out to be since he brought me here. Even without being able to talk to him, he's responded to every single 'no' I gave him.

If I refuse his heat, he'll let me. But that's what you call cutting off your nose to spite your face. I'm freezing, he's warm, and I'm going to take him up on his offer.

Reaching up, I grab his hand. Careful not to prick myself on the points of his claws, I wrap my fingers around his massive thumb and give him a gentle tug. It takes him a second to understand what I want. From the way his lips turn down, he obviously thinks I'm trying to stop him from touching me. Slowly, regretfully, he pulls his hand away from my face.

But when I don't release his thumb, instead taking his arm between two of mine, he goes still.

"Bed," I say. I use my free hand to wave at it.

"Hinae," he says. "Loki i Ken-dee hinae?"

Does that mean 'bed'? I'm thinking it does when he follows my lead, climbing up into the dip in the center of the bed with me.

I'm still holding onto his arm. Looking over at him, I ask, "Is this okay?"

Loki doesn't understand me. No surprise. But if he's offering to be my personal heater, it's the least he can do for me after stealing me. I'm not about to sleep with him again—but I will sleep next to him.

I didn't really want to sleep on the floor.

Squeezing his arm, I nod. "Yes? Kennedy, yes?"

He rumbles in pleasure.

There's no other way to describe the noise he makes. Unlike some of his earlier frustrated grunts and growls, my beastly monster's eyes go impossibly brighter as his chest seems to vibrate—and all because I squeezed one of his big arms between mine, trying to steal as much of his heat as I possibly could.

Little things make him happy, I see.

Then again, as Freya worms her way between us, sleeping between our bodies—and Loki doesn't try to shoo her away—I realize that little things make me happy, too.

———

WHEN I WAKE UP THE NEXT MORNING, IT TAKES ME A moment to realize where I am.

It's darker than it should be. That's not right. I'm

rested, like I've slept for hours. It can't still be night now.

I also shouldn't be cuddled up against a big, hard body.

Loki's bright eyes are on a dimmer. I didn't know he could control them. To keep from disturbing my rest, they're barely glowing—until he sees that I'm awake. Lips curving, his eyes light up.

My heart jolts, breath catching in my throat as I pop up into a sitting position.

Everything comes rushing back to me. The book. Waking up to find him stalking around my bedroom. The way he pulled me into the closet. The strange portal. The trip to his two-room shelter. Freya.

Freya.

Her fur brushes against my ankle. My movement disturbed her and she lifts her head, chittering softly before she curls up again.

I'm up. She still wants her sleep. And Loki?

I don't think he slept at all.

In a throaty voice, aware of how intently he's staring at me, I murmur, "Good morning."

"Ken-dee mi."

His hand hovers over my cheek. He wants to touch me, though he's not sure if I'll welcome him.

I want to. The urge to tip my head forehead, pressing my skin against his heated palm is almost overwhelming. If I'm going to be stuck here, I should take comfort where I can get it.

If only his didn't come with strings attached.

I might have woken up facing Loki, curled up against him, but I purposely fell asleep with my back to him. Despite how tired I was, I was still viscerally aware of where he was at all times. His heat warmed my skin, and while he didn't try to initiate sex again, he climbed into the bed naked. We might both be ignoring his monster dick. No matter how I tried to angle my hips away from his groin, I couldn't avoid bumping into it.

I will admit one thing. Once I put my foot down, Loki is a perfect gentleman. Of course, it's easy for him to back off when we've already slept together. He might think it's inevitable that we will again. All he has to do is wait.

He can wait all he wants. That's not my style.

He's all I have. I'm assuming he's not the only of his kind, but for whatever reason, when I read that spell, he's the one who answered. He brought me back home with him. I have a pretty solid guess *why*, but until we can actually communicate with each other, guessing is all I can do.

I need to understand his motives. Is it just sex? Because he can get the fuck out of here with that. As big and ferocious-looking as he is, he's been kind. I couldn't have asked for a more attentive captor if I had to be kidnapped. Loki's been insistent on taking care of me, and I'm going to let him.

And then, when we can finally communicate, I'm

going to convince him that I belong back in the human world.

First things first. We need to communicate.

Well. Before I decided to be a bookseller, I played around with the idea of being an English teacher instead.

Looks like I'm going to get the chance.

CHAPTER 9
KISS

KENNEDY

Tyler once accused me of not knowing what I wanted. I didn't understand what he meant. I made it clear that my goal was to open my bookshop, get married, have kids. It was my life's plan.

I've *always* known what I wanted.

Until a seven-foot-tall monster with two sets of horns and a sexy smile stalked into my life and carried me kicking and screaming into his.

At least I know where I am now. If I'm understanding Loki right, this shadowy world is known as Sombra. Pretty obvious in retrospect, right? *Grimoire du Sombra*… grimoire of Sombra.

Sombra's grimoire.

Do I know *what* Sombra is? Nope. I did learn that

there are more of his kind of monster who live here, though Loki's eyes flare when I make a miming gesture asking if we have neighbors. I decided to take that as a no. Wherever we are, we're off the Sombra grid, I bet.

At least we have water and a toilet. It could've been worse.

Just like I could've been taken hostage by a monster more interested in getting into my nonexistent panties than trying his best to make me feel comfortable in his small home.

I keep expecting him to try again. To crook his finger or even take hold of his cock and start stroking like he did my first day here. He doesn't. As though he finally got it through his thick skull that I'm not interested in banging him, he ignores his constant erection as we begin to have as normal a routine as you can have after being kidnapped by a monster.

And when I find myself sneaking glances at his dick more than I should, I finally understand what my ex was getting at. Because while my dreams of love and kids in the future haven't changed, I kind of… I kind of start seeing myself with Loki.

Crazy, isn't it? Over the last two weeks together, we've exchanged enough words that we can have a stilted conversation together. Is that enough to throw away my old life for one in the shadows?

For the first time in a long time, I don't know *what* I want…

It's not all roses here. There are good days and there are bad days. Most of the bad days are when I get frustrated and just need my space. As if he can sense when I'm at the end of my rope, Loki disappears into the shadows for hours until he slinks back into our room.

He always has a gift for me. Fiery flowers and shards of volcanic glass that glimmer in the floating, magic lights. Strangely black plants that made me nervous, but that Freya devoured. When Loki took one of the stems, coyly waving it in front of my face, I eventually ate it and almost moaned when it tasted like popcorn of all things.

After that, he finds me other edible flowers and plants. Some sweet, some savory, some that tasted like straight grass, I'm a lot happier when my meals aren't entirely hunks of seared meat.

I know what he's doing, too. He's courting me. An old-fashioned term for my monster, but it fits. Providing for me, too.

Showing me he could be a good partner.

How can I not start falling for him?

One thing I can't get him to understand is how gross I started to feel about a week after he brought me here. There was a point where I'd kill for a shower. Every time Loki leaves the house, he brings back a layer of dust with him. He doesn't need to bathe. Shifting forms burns off any dirt or—after a hunt— blood that might have clung to him.

Not me. I passed ripe a few days after my arrival, and when I finally accept that he isn't hiding a bathtub around here, I start to wash up using the water tube. Rinsing my hair was pretty easy, even if I don't have anything to cleanse it with.

When my temper gets the better of me, I think about how much I probably stink without any soap. Loki wanted to take me? To keep me? Let him learn how smelly a human can get when there's no deodorant and her personal heated blanket has her sweating like a pig.

He likes it. When I'm sure I'm rank, he nuzzles my armpit and sighs happily.

That doesn't mean I'm not sick and tired of my dress. And on one of my worst days, I think about ripping it off, shoving it at Loki to burn, while stomping around in my birthday suit. He does. Why can't I?

Before it gets to that point, Loki picks up on just how much I'm beginning to hate the printed dress I yanked on so many days ago.

One day, after another language lesson, I'm plucking idly at a loose thread on my dusty skirt —*again*—when his brow furrows in concentration.

The air grows warm. That catches my attention. With his hand outstretched in front of him, I watch as he conjures something.

I've gotten used to these small displays of magic. It's still amazing. Whether it's flames to cook our meat or a comb for me to brush my tangled hair, the way he creates things out of nothing is amazing.

Even more amazing is his surprised yet proud expression every time he accomplishes it.

Whatever he's conjuring now looks like shadows, though it flows like a more tangible fabric as he weaves magic, creating—

A *dress*.

It's a black, shadowy dress that can finally replace the golden yellow sundress that's turned a dingy grey over the last week, and I'm suddenly ecstatic.

I don't know how he does it. I don't care. When he holds the dress out to me, I squeal and, before I even think of changing, I throw myself at Loki.

My hands go around his middle. Squeezing him tightly, I tilt my head back so that I can meet his glowing white eyes. "Thank you, Loki. Thank you so— *oh*."

"Uxor mi," he breathes, lifting his hand slowly toward my face.

It's the expression on his that has my breath catching in my throat.

I don't even know when he stopped looking like a monster to me. In the days since Loki appeared in my life, almost like he was tailor-made for me—even if he is some kind of a monster from a world of shadows—I've gotten used to his features. I barely notice the slight ridges over his long nose, or the four polished horns arcing over his head until the flickering lights reflect off of them. Whether he's standing there, solid and in his red skin, or going as dark as night with only his glowing white eyes breaking up his shadowy form, he's just… he's just *Loki*.

Right now he's solid, his long hair falling in front of his broad shoulders as he tucks his chin into his wide chest, staring down at me. The points of his fangs dig into his lush bottom lip as his hard features seem to soften.

I've seen him possessive. I've seen him lusty. I've seen him crook a claw, a seductive twist to his smile, as he called me to him. I've seen him curious. I've seen him confused. When we couldn't really talk to each other with words, I had to adapt. Between body language and reading his expressions like they're an open book written just for me, I had to learn my big demon.

I'm still learning, too, and every day is another revelation.

Like how I'm suddenly really curious to find out what he tastes like…

"Loki…"

With the curve of his claw, he tucks my hair behind my ear. His fingertip brushes against the shell. Regardless of his temperature, the gentle caress burns.

So does the rest of me.

I've slept with him. He had his mouth and his

those fangs on my most private parts. And, yet, it's that touch that has me revving in place.

I drop my gaze from his eyes to his mouth. I'm not so sure why. It just seems the thing to do.

It hits me that we've never kissed. He's bumped my cheek, as if he knows our faces can touch as intimately as other parts of our bodies. Whether pressing lips together or stroking tongues is something that his people do or not, I never put myself in a position where I wanted to try.

Until now.

My lips part. Rising up on my tiptoes, I give him an opened-mouth kiss on the closest part of him I can reach. It's near one rust-colored nipple. I kiss him, and he groans.

"Kiss," I say.

Lifting my hand, I gesture for him to bow his head, bringing his lips closer to mine. Following my lead, eager to see what I'm going to do next, Loki does. I swipe my mouth across his, not remembering his fangs until I'm pulling back, then diving back in to pepper small kisses at the corner of his mouth.

I trust him. He won't hurt me, and his fangs are just another part of him like his fingers or his cock. Licking the seam of his lips, pushing insistently with the tip of my tongue, I wait to see if he'll let me in— or if he'll think what I'm doing is strange.

Strange or not, Loki opens his mouth, letting my tongue delve right in.

His mouth is as hot as the rest of him, making me realize how cold I must be in comparison. He doesn't mind, though. Following the rhythm of my motion, he kisses me back. His inexperience is obvious. I don't care. There's something charming in the way Loki kisses.

When I pull back, he growls softly in his throat, following my mouth.

I pat his chest.

"Ken-dee?"

"Kiss," I tell him again. Might as well take the time to teach him the word to go along with it. "Kiss."

"Kiss," he echoes and leans in to brush his lips against mine again.

In so many ways, my monster proves to be a fast learner.

LOKI

My Ken-dee is healing me.

Just having her in my sight is enough to beat back the worst of the shadows. When she allows me to touch her, they nearly disappear.

She has not invited me to mate her again no matter how I scent her cunt growing ready for me. But she allows me to kiss her, and I accept each lip touch as eagerly as the last.

Especially since I started to doubt she would ever

let me touch her again after I carried her through the portal into Sombra.

I was a selfish male. I know this now. So consumed with recognizing that she was my mate, I didn't think to ask if she would come with me. I didn't want to risk breaking Duke Haures's first law. The idea of leaving her behind never occurred to me. She was mine, and that meant she had to come with me.

She's content now. Happier after I removed the human skull from our sleeping quarters. The only time I ever scented fear coming from my mate was when she saw the smooth skull. She must have thought I hunted her kind.

I hunt the shadow vermin and the beasts. I've never seen a human before my Ken-dee and I would never use my claws against her people. I do my best to make sure she understands this.

The ungez she's claimed as hers counts as her people. No matter how my mouth waters, I do not eat it. I feed it instead, sharing the meat and plants I gather for my mate with her 'pet'.

My mate is sweet. She is kind. Watching her tend to the vermin has my chest puffing out. As gentle and protective as she is over the creature, I can only imagine what a good mother she'll be when we have offspring.

I've always wanted a family of my own. Spawn that's part Loki, part Ken-dee. Finding my mate should have meant that I would have one, though it's been close to a cycle now and I have yet to gather enough essence to finalize my mate bond with Ken-dee.

I'm healing. Every day with Ken-dee makes me a better Sombra demon. When I'm whole enough that I have my soul back, I will give it to her. She will know me and my thoughts. Understand that everything I do, I do for her. If I can give essence, I can accept it, and I will finally know all of my clever little mate.

For now, she sits with me. Sleeps beside me, taking the warmth I so freely offer her. She teaches me as I teach her. It's slow going, reminding me of my early days at the School of Mages when every lesson seemed impossible, but I'm a devoted pupil.

If I can't learn her through her essence, I will learn her in other ways.

My Ken-dee is my favorite subject.

I always knew I would love my mate. The gods set aside one female in all the worlds for me, but even they could not foresee how easily I would grow to need having one small human close.

She teases me in the few words we share. Delights with me when her ungez snuggles between us, the creature's tail whipping Ken-dee's belly, its claws kneading my demon chest. When I conjure her a comb after seeing her struggle to drag her fingers through her watered hair, she gives me an embrace— a 'hug'—and parks me down in front of her to comb my hair after she finishes hers.

Starting the next time she waters her hair, I insist on combing hers. She still combs mine. Knowing she gets enjoyment from running a bone comb through my long hair has me aching to turn around, pick her up, and lay her out on our bed.

But I won't. Not until she gives me a sign that she is ready to welcome me once more. She did so easily once, dazed by the mate bond snapping into place between us. I will relish taking her again when I know I've earned her heart.

I am close. With every day, her affection for me grows. I work hard for her favor. Ken-dee deserves an honorable male. I strive to be one.

Maybe if she had been born before I was lost, I could have.

Because though I am better than I once was, there is a difference between being a demon and going demonic—and I live with the repercussions of the second every single day.

I was born a proud Sombra demon. But going demonic... walking into the shadows not caring whether they defeated me or I joined them... that didn't happen until it was too late for me to get control of myself.

And it was all because of my magic, and my desire to find my mate.

In Sombra, everyone does their part. The great Duke Haures is our ruler, the male who has lorded over the capital city for two thousand years. We have clan leaders. Hunters. Trades demons. Spawn minders. Teachers. Artists, and butchers. Weavers of both fabrics and shadows. Soldiers. Builders.

And, of course, mages.

Born with the tell-tale purple eyes, I knew I was always destined to be a mage. I was also the only demon born in my clan who came out of my mother's womb with two pairs of nubs on my brow. Double horns are the mark of a powerful demon. I could have been a fierce fighter—and I am—but the magic inside of me sealed my fate. I would be a mage, and that meant I had to leave Arith, the clan of my kin, to train.

Once I was of age, I left for Marvo, the oasis in the center of Sombra, where I was taught by the most powerful mage of our age. The youngest to learn under Sammael, I'd only seen two centuries then. Little more than a spawn when I came to learn magic in the capital, finding my mate had been the last thing on my mind.

But as I studied, I also matured. I hadn't seen a female since I left Arith—since only males in Sombra can be born as mages, there were none in our quarters—but I started to dream of the day I found her.

She would love me instantly as I love her. She would lust for me, her demoness instincts leading her to claim me and bond with me as soon as our eyes met.

Ken-dee is no demoness. She is one of the fabled

humans. She called me to her, though I didn't answer her summons straight away. Proving that humans are as powerful as the sweet demonesses from Soleil only without any horns to protect them, we mated, forming our bond, and that's when I was reminded of what I lost by going fully demonic.

The broken demons have no essence. No soul.

I have my Ken-dee now. I'll always have her.

But without an essence exchange, I can't delve into her mind. Into her memories. I know not what she thinks of me, or if she loves me as much as I would give anything for one of her smiles.

I survived the shadows. I am resilient. I am determined.

And I will continue to learn her on my own until I'm whole enough to offer her my essence.

There's no hurry. We are safe in my home. She's made no move to leave either of the rooms, content to stay with her ungez when I must go to hunt and reinforce my territorial markings.

We sleep in the same bed every night, though my Ken-dee does not want to mate. As much as I'd love to worship her cunt like she allowed back in her realm, I do as she says. She is my mate, our bond present if not finalized, and I will wait until she wants to make me hers once more.

Because finally, as I'm approaching my fifth century, I've learned patience—and I did it for my heart.

But just because I cannot share myself with her, I know that she is the only female in all the worlds who owns my heart. She *is* my heart.

And though she knows as much Sombran as I've learned of her human language, I wait until she's softly snoring to tell her the same thing I've done every night since I found her before I did.

"My soul will be yours," I whisper, trailing a claw down her soft cheek. My Ken-dee is soft everywhere. "My heart is in your hands. Our lives will be forever intertwined." I vow it. More than a promise, it is my solemn vow. "I give myself to you. I give you everything."

Everything, it seems, except for my essence.

LOKI

I've learned much about my sweet mate since I brought her to my home, including how humans need an awful lot of rest.

In the shadows, to sleep is to be vulnerable. I mark my immediate territory to ward off predators, though there are some that are either too stupid or foolhardy to challenge a demon male. I also find myself losing myself if I sleep too long. When I was whole, I only needed a few hours recharge to be rested. Now? I can go many moons without shutting down.

I must watch Ken-dee. Keeping her safe and protected is my priority. I laid down beside her in the beginning because she wasn't used to the shadows' chilly bite. Seeing how she was pleased when I tapped into my growing well of magic and conjured her a new covering, I did the same and wove her a blanket out of shadows.

She was pleased, yet still invited me to lie down beside her whenever she slumbered.

It was inevitable that, eventually, I would need to close my eyes as well. I'd gone as long as I could without resting. My body followed her into slumber, my hand settling on her waist so that, even while my eyes were away from her, I still kept that connection.

When I finally come out of my rest, that my hand is laying flat against the sheet instead of on Kend-ee has me bolting out of the bed. Breathing in deep, I search for her scent. Panic floods my form when I find it and it is old.

I fell asleep as a demon. To stay in a shadow near Ken-dee is too much of a temptation. I'm more sensitive in that form. One accidental brush against Ken-dee and I nearly erupt right on the floor.

No. It is better to stay tangible where I'm as solid as she. She seems to prefer it, too. In my demon form, I scent her cunt growing wet far more often than when I melt into the darkness.

Once I sense that my Ken-dee is gone? Rage replaces the panic and I instantly turn shadow. I tamp it down, wrangling control over my dark side, but I force the change further, becoming mist.

It'll be easier and faster to follow after Ken-dee

like this once I streak into the water room and see that the door to the outside is open and my mate is missing.

If she had my essence but we did not finalize our mate bond, she could not go far. It's built into our mating ritual, just like the mate sickness. The gods will do anything to push two of their fated mates together. Sombra demons *are* shadow. Until our bond is secure, we must stay within a short distance of our intended mate.

I don't want my Ken-dee to suffer from mate sickness. Once I thought I would take any excuse I could find to lay my hands on her. That's changed. I want to earn that honor along with her heart. Touching her to ease the burn caused by mate sickness would be pleasurable, but ultimately not satisfying for either of us.

Do I wish that I could use a mate bond to follow after her? Desperately. I have some magic, but I failed with the matefinder spell once before; I won't risk casting it again, not when my magic store is still so low. Since I have no other choice, I must rely on my tracking and hunting skills to find her.

Where could she have gone? Why would she have left me?

I've done everything to prove that I am the best male for her. And she left me.

I will find her. If only to keep her safe from the dangers lurking in the shadows, I will find Ken-dee.

In this form, I can fly. Mages prefer portal travel because it is faster, but every Sombra demon can channel their mist and launch themself forward. It's why village houses have circles cut into the ceilings for a quick escape instead of wasting energy passing through it.

Prepared to take off, I stop when I catch Ken-dee's scent on the breeze. Worse, it's mixed with a familiar predator's musk.

No.

I stopped searching for the arkoda. With Ken-dee in my home, I no longer thought about those long moons, tracking the beast.

That was my mistake. So was not finding the words to explain to my mate that the shadows were too dangerous for her to chance.

But I didn't, and now the arkoda found her.

Ken-dee's not moving. Paralyzed with fright, she's standing still in the shadows as the arkoda circles her. The massive beast has fallen forward, lumbering on all fours, patient because his prey presents no threat. He's playing with her. Drinking in her fright before he finishes his kill.

And he will.

I killed his mate. He will attempt to slaughter mine.

Never.

I roar. The action is both calculated as it is instinctive. I want the arkoda to come after me instead of

Ken-dee.

I'm the bigger threat. The bigger prize. There is more meat on my bones, and that means nothing when he recognizes me as the demon responsible for hunting his mate.

He knows my musk and I know his.

The arkoda echoes my roar. It's lower, so loud the ground beneath my shadow form.

"Holysheet, holy*sheet.*" Ken-dee collapses to the ash. Her legs finally fail to hold her slight weight. "Loki, ruhn!"

She says my name. I don't know what else she tells me. Warning me about the arkoda, perhaps, but there's something else she doesn't know.

The beast would've killed her, but it can also destroy me.

Of all the creatures in the shadows, the arkoda is the closest to the demon race. Intelligent and fierce, the arkoda was designed to cull an immortal race. They're the duke of Sombra's pets. When he wants to execute a demon, he sends them to the shadows.

He sends them to the arkoda.

It's part of the reason why I chased it for so many moons. So lost, I did not fear death. I searched for it, ready to prove my might or succumb to the beast.

But that was before. Now? I won't let anyone or anything hurt my mate.

Ken-dee is mine. And I will survive if only to

make sure she makes it back to my shack without anything else targeting her as prey.

The last time I tracked an arkoda, I was careful in my hunt. In my approach. Not now. Not with Ken-dee so close. Giving myself over to the most primal side of any Sombra demon, I make myself as big as possible, going as solid as I can while wearing my shadows, and lunge at the arkoda.

The arkoda was playing with Ken-dee. With me? He goes straight for the kill. That works to my advantage. He's reckless, furious, eager to rend me from chest to gut.

I let him try, using all of my strength to grab and tear one of his front legs until it's hanging off its body. Unlike Sombra demons, the predators and the prey who lurk in the shadows have only one form. They might look like they're transparent, but it's like Ken-dee's ungez. They're solid, and I risk his claws in order to get close enough to attack.

Mine are just as sharp. Once his front leg is useless, he's down to one set of claws. I have two, plus I am a two-horn. The fight is over within a few terrible seconds.

I have the beast on his back, belly up in no time.

And I think: I used my claws to rip the arkoda's female to pieces. Raising my hand high, I will do the same to him—

—until Ken-dee gasps.

My hand stills. Turning behind me, I see my

human mate crouched in the dirt, wee hands clamped over her mouth.

A fresh wave of the fear scent clings to her.

Is she afraid of *me*?

I want her to see her male as powerful. I am a two-horn, strong and brave. But she's as frightened of me as she was the arkoda.

To my Ken-dee, I am now the beast.

No. *No.* I tamp down the shadows. I won't allow them to take me. I've done so much to claw back my soul, searching for a drop of essence to give my mate. I won't sacrifice it, hunt or no hunt.

Baring my fangs at the dazed arkoda, I show him mercy while making sure the beast knows better than to ever come sniffing around my mate again.

"Go," I snarl, slashing my arm in the space in front of me. "And know that the only reason I spare you is because a life without your mate is worse than a quick death."

Is the arkoda intelligent enough to understand Sombran? I'm not sure, but he hauls his bulk off of the ash, lumbering away as quickly as it can with his mangled foreleg before I change my mind about letting it go.

However, when I wait until it's melted into the shadows before turning on my heel to face my mate, I know that I made the right choice. The fear scent has faded, her face torn between pride and… and—

She stumbles to her feet, tripping over them, trembling in fear and concern. "Loki? Loki! U ok?"

I subdued the arkoda in my shadow form. While it attempted to rend me with its claws, I wanted the victory more. As a demon, I might have been hurt. In shadow, I'm fine.

"Worry not, my mate. Come. Let's go home."

She knows that word. I taught her it so that she knew my shack was her home.

Instead of agreeing, she digs her heels into the ash. "No. Ineedurhelp," she says in English before saying in Sombran, "Help!"

Help? "Ken-dee?"

She points into the darkness. "Itz Freya. Loki help Freya."

I know that word, too. *Freya*. The ungez. Her companion.

Suddenly, I understand. Somehow the vermin has found its way outside. I thought it was attached to Ken-dee, but ungez are wild. If the shadows beckoned it, the creature might have answered.

And my sweet mate would have worried and gone searching for it until the arkoda got in her way.

Arkoda gobble ungez by the dozen. If Ken-dee's companion caught the scent of the arkoda stalking nearby, it would have found somewhere to hide... if it managed to avoid the arkoda's maw.

I refuse to leave Ken-dee to the mercy of other predators. Tucking her into my side, ignoring her protests, I guide her back to the shack before gently nudging her inside.

She hesitates inside the first room. "Watbout Freya?"

I gesture for her to go further inside, then use two of my horns to motion that I am going to return to the shadows to search for the ungez.

Ken-dee goes up on her tiptoes, pursing her lips. I recognize this. Whenever Ken-dee does that, she wants a 'kiss'.

I am happy to take it with me before I ease the door to my home open before stalking back out into the shadows.

After living with the ungez for many moons, I know the creature's scent as well as Ken-dee's. Since it imprinted on my mate, it smells of her.

I know Ken-dee's scent anywhere. By following that, I can find the ungez for my mate.

I break further into the shadows. For those used to them, they fade enough so that we can use the landscape as I guide. It's how I can track and can hunt, and it's how I plan on retrieving the ungez for Ken-dee.

Most of this part of Sombra is dotted with ash trees. Impossibly black, gnarled and bare, they are covered in soot from the days before the shadows on the edge of Sombra advanced this far. Once they burned, now they stand twisted, warped by the shadows.

The ungez prefer to make their nests in the branches and the knots of those trees. I search them, knowing I'm close when Ken-dee's sweet scent wraps around my senses.

My ears twitch. There are plenty of ungez that scatter around this part of the shadows, but when I hear the familiar chittering as I continue to follow my mate's scent, I'm certain I have discovered its hiding place.

Like I expected, it's tucked deep inside of a knot on a towering ash tree.

"Come, little creature. My Ken-dee misses you." I click my tongue against my fang. "Come to Loki."

It must recognize my scent as well. After a few moments, the ungez pops its head out of the knot, its nose twitching. When I hold out my palm, it jumps onto it, wrapping its tail around my wrist.

I trap it beneath my claw. Even if it decides to run off, it no longer can.

With Ken-dee's companion in hand, I start to turn back toward the shack. As I do, another wave of the arkoda's musk filters in front of my nose.

He is near, I realize. And Ken-dee is not in sight to watch me complete the hunt.

For a moment, I think about shoving the ungez back in the knot and stalking off after the wounded arkoda. It will regenerate if left in the shadows, but not if I finish what I started.

Once, the satisfaction of besting the arkoda would

have drawn me out of my madness and my weariness for a time.

But that was before I found my Ken-dee.

If the arkoda approaches my territory again, I might have to. For now, my mate is waiting for me and this vermin.

CHAPTER 11
KENN-UH-DEE

LOKI

The sound of Ken-dee's delighted squeal when I hand her the ungez is enough to soothe the last of the fear of losing her from my chest. Until she is immortal and nothing is left to threaten, it shall return, but for now I am just pleased that I could make her smile so widely up at me.

"Tanku Loki." She lifts her companion to her nose, nuzzling past the shadowy fur of the critter. "Freya ubadgurl. Dontdodat gen, k?"

She's still smiling, even if her tone sounds slightly scolding. Again, she glances up at me but, this time, her smile dips.

It's not quite a frown, but it's close.

"Loki," she breathes out. "Ur*eyez*."

Before, she was talking to the ungez. Now she's

139

addressing me, but I do not understand. So, like I do when she's trying to teach me her language—or learn mine—and I struggle with a word, I shake my head.

Giving the ungez one last snuggle, she sets it down on the floor. Chirping happily as if its escape didn't nearly cost my mate her mortal life, it scampers around the room. And it did that. Until I have claimed Kennedy fully, with both the essence exchange and the mate's promise, she won't share my immortality. She could have died, and all for an ungez.

Hm. Perhaps I should have left it in the knot...

Ken-dee clears her throat, snaring my attention. One look at her delicate features and I take back that thought. To make my mate smile the way she did when I handed her the ungez, I would have wrestled a hundred arkoda.

I return her grin with a crooked one of my own.

She's staring up at me. I want her to smile again. She does not. Instead, she taps the side of her face, her pointer finger gesturing at one of her dark, dim eyes, then turns it on me.

Ah. She was referring to my eyes before.

"I know they are bright and yours are dim. I don't mind. I love you just as you are."

I love her, and if the arkoda had hunted Ken-dee before I knew she was gone, I could have lost her.

Ah. I was right. The fear is back.

I lift my hand, rubbing my chest with the heel.

Our bond is there, a reminder that she's mine though I often wonder if she knows that. It's grown stronger every day that I've loved her, grown thicker every time I whisper the mate's promise to her as she sleeps, and I only wish that she feels it, too.

And maybe she does. Because Ken-dee? She's rubbing the same spot on her own chest with her fingertips.

"Loki?"

My name is a question that I cannot answer for her.

Instead, I open my arms up. I feel as though, immortal demon or not, if I don't touch her, I might die.

"Please," I say. "Let me hold you, my mate."

None of those are words that we've taught each other. She doesn't need to be able to translate what I'm saying to know what I'm asking of her.

Without any hesitation, she walks right into my embrace.

I close my arms around her.

It starts out innocently enough. As if she's remembering my quick fight with the arkoda, she's running her hands over my body. Her breath is a chilly exhale against my overheated flesh when she doesn't find any injuries. It is nearly impossible to hurt a Somdra demon in his shadow form, so I knew she wouldn't.

But I didn't know that she would continue her exploration of my body until my sweet human mate does the last thing I ever expected: Ken-dee boldly grabs my cock.

A roar begs to escape my throat. Only knowing that I would never forgive myself if I frightened her again has me forcing it back.

Instead, in a strangled voice, I say, "Ken-dee?"

She releases my cock, backing up until she bumps against the bed. Giving me the wicked grin she wore the night she summoned me to her quarters, she pats the top of the sheet with the flat of her hand.

I gulp, not daring to believe she's offering me anything other than sleeping beside her, sharing with her my heat.

And then she says, "Uxor mi," in such an inviting tone, I almost spill seed without even touching her.

'My mate'. For the first time, Ken-dee just called me her mate.

She isn't ready to sleep. She's ready to mate.

And so am I.

I am naked. With a wave of my hand, her shadow coverings disappear instantly.

I don't know what stuns me more: seeing her heaving breasts, her enticing curves, and the thatch of hair on her cunt already slick with her need, or how easily I was able to use magic to banish the shadows.

In Sombra, we have seamstresses who weave fabric and make coverings that last. For shadow coverings, any demon can call forth their shadows and use them to conceal their bodies. Being naked in front of another is an honor reserved for only a mate. No female has ever seen me unclothed until my Ken-dee, and they never shall.

That I spent so long uncovered in the shadows was a mark of how fully demonic I went. When I found my mate, there was no need. I could have if she told me she preferred me to be covered, but since I caught Ken-dee eyeing my cock, I didn't want to hide it from her.

My cock, like every other part of me, belongs to my female.

But to weave shadows to dress another? That's something only a mage can do. It took more effort than I used in many a cycle when I created the shadow covering for Ken-dee, but vanishing it?

It happened so easily, I gawk at her.

Or maybe I gawk because she's a vision before me.

It takes Ken-dee a moment to notice that she's bare. Glancing down, throwing her arm over her breasts, she squeals my name.

I pause, halfway toward grabbing her. "No?" It's the human sound that tells me Ken-dee doesn't want me to do something. "Loki Ken-dee no?"

"DatsnotwatImeant," she says.

I tilt my head. My hand twitches, sliding over to my hard cock. If she does not want to mate, I cannot wait to go to the toilet to take my release like I've done countless times so that I do not pressure her into giving me what I have not earned.

But I cannot reach for her so long as she says the 'no' sound.

As much magic as my mortal mate has, her eyes do not glow the same way the demons do. And, yet, when she juts her chin, showing off the smooth column of her colorless throat, they seem to shine as she says, "Loki Kennedy *yes*."

That's all the permission I need before I have her under me.

I purposely stay in my shadows. The first time I ever mated Ken-dee, I worried about her size. Demonesses match a demon's height and bulk. Strong and sturdy, they can easily take their male's cock. I knew instinctively that my human was my mate. The gods wouldn't have given me a female I could not mate or breed.

But she was small, and a demon is large. To make it so we could fit easily, I stayed to my shadows during our first mating so that I could adjust the size of my cock to her cunt. That I'm doubly as sensitive mating in my shadows was just a plus.

I want to taste her again. I want to nuzzle her breast and take her nipple between my lips. I want to feed my cock past hers so that she can know my taste. I want to sit on my backside while my Ken-dee rides me, or put her on her hands and knees so that I can possess every inch of her...

I want it all, but because I'm so afraid she'll push me away, I settle for bracing one hand near her shoulder, the other grabbing my cock and quickly lodging the head inside of her.

There's not as much resistance now as there was during our first mating. She's breathing quick, a combination of need and excitement, but as I push harder, feeding her more of my cock, she's running her hands over my chest.

It's bare. As soon as Ken-dee is my forever mate, I will carve her name in my chest and pour enchanted silver into the wounds so that all in Sombra know that I am owned by her.

For now, I settle on showing my female that she made no mistake when she called me her mate at last.

She writhes beneath me as I thrust, making sure she can feel my shadows and my cock stretching her cunt from the inside out. I refuse to stop until I feel her tightening around me, like a vice that never wants to let me go.

Only then do I find my own pleasure.

As I release my seed inside of her cunt, I take her head between my palms. Holding her in place as she keens beneath me, cool fingers absently stroking my sides, I press my brow against hers.

A spark passes between us. It's instinctive. I didn't mean to do it because I didn't think I could. I barely am aware that I *did*. I only wanted to hold her, to love her, to make her understand that there is nothing I won't do for her.

"My mate." I'm panting, pinning her on my cock even as I'm careful not to lay my weight on her. She's so small. I want to cocoon her, brushing her with my shadows, breathing her in as I murmur in Sombran to her. "My beautiful mate. My heart. I love you so much."

Ken-dee stiffens. Her fingers dip into my side.

"What did you just say?"

I extend my elbows, rising up so that I can see her face.

She looks as shocked as I feel.

Because my mate? She just spoke to me in fluent Sombran.

KENNEDY

Still buried to the hilt inside of me, Loki is staring at me like a slack-jawed idiot.

He has no reason to. I'm the one who might have just lost their mind. Because, unless I'm imagining it, Loki said something to me in Sombran *and I understood him*.

More than that, I responded *in his language*.

What just happened? *How* did that happen? I've worked so hard to learn a handful of words and, suddenly, he gives me his dick again and now I know Sombran?

Now I know that his language is *called* Sombran?

Did he know that would happen? Was that why he was so insistent in the beginning that we fuck again? Is that how it works here?

For some reason, the word 'essence' pops into my brain. I shove it out, then try to shove Loki away from me.

Only one works. I forget all about 'essence' while struggling to move Loki an inch.

I push his chest again. "Get off me."

He frowns.

"Get off me!"

That's what I meant to say. The words that I shout aren't in English, but like before, I understand them instinctively.

I just spoke in Loki's demon language again. Without even meaning to, I switched from English to Sombran.

Are you kidding me?

I don't think that's what has him rising up, pushing his big body off of mine. You ask me, he doesn't look surprised at all that I'm suddenly fluent. Oh, no. It's the pitch of my voice 'cause I'm two seconds away from freaking out. The way I shouted at him to get off.

He goes. Withdrawing his cock slowly, I swallow my traitorous moan as he manages to hit nearly every damn nerve ending on his way out. His expression still bewildered if less wild than before, he shifts to the other side of the bed.

Scrambling up and off of it, I move out of his reach while I try to process what just happened.

It all started with that… that *thing*. The scary beast thing that attacked me when I went searching for Freya.

That part was my fault. With Loki fast asleep for the first time since I've known him, my curiosity got the better of me. I had this strange urge to peek my head out of the only door in his home, getting a better look at the shadow world of Sombra.

I never expected Freya to dart outside, or that I'd discover what other types of creatures live out in the dark.

Freya is a squirrel-cat. That *thing* was a bear-goat on steroids. If Loki hadn't woken up in time to come after me, he would've had another human skull for his collection.

But he did. As though he could sense I was in trouble, he came in the nick of time—but there was only one thing I kept thinking about during the fight, then after, when Loki showed he has a soft side and let the big beast go.

And that was this: he could have *died*.

He's all I have to rely on in this terrifying world, but I also have to admit that I'm fooling myself if I say that's the only reason why I can't even fathom the idea of him being killed by that massive shadow beast.

I like him. I have feelings for him that have been able to grow without the added complication of sex. Lord knows we're already compatible in that department, but he's treated me so well after kidnapping me that—and I know this smacks of Stockholm Syndrome or something—I can't help but be drawn to him.

And then he saved me and Freya, and all I could think about once we were safe was getting him into bed.

I remember once reading that adrenaline can be an aphrodisiac. Danger-banging is definitely a thing. If not that, he went after Freya. My little squirrel-cat that means so much to me but is a nuisance to Loki, and he didn't even hesitate.

I had been looking for a reason to let down my guard. To stop this no-sex thing I accidentally started those first days when I honestly didn't want to reward him for taking me. Then I started to get used to living with him, learning him, teaching him, and... yeah. I've been dying to fuck him again.

I just never imagined that, when I did, I'd suddenly be able to understand my monster—

No, I correct. He's not a monster. He's a demon. A proud Sombran demon.

I already knew we were in Sombra. But Loki's home is built on the edge of the shadows to be exact and, holy shit, how do I suddenly know all of that?

"Ken-dee?"

"It's Kennedy," I snap. It just comes out. "My name is Kenn-uh-dee."

I never both correcting him before because it didn't matter. Suddenly, it *does*.

Loki works his jaw. "Kennedy?"

Look at that. All this time and he couldn't get it, but as soon as I get a download of his demon language in my brain, he finally can?

For some reason, that makes me even more angry.

Damn it. Where's a high heel when you need one?

CHAPTER 12
KENNEDY KILLS LOKI

KENNEDY

My first instinct is to run back outside if only to get away from that look on the demon's face.

Of course, then I have a flash of the beast—

Arkoda, my mind supplies.

Wonderful. Two seconds ago, I was happy thinking of that thing as a snarling bear beast, and now I know what the Sombrans call it.

Well, whatever that thing is, it might still be out there. It might have friends.

No, thanks.

I'm still the type of woman who needs space to process her emotions so that she can make decisions. They're often rash decisions, not gonna lie, but I make them and I stand by them.

That might not be so easy right now. First of all, the farthest I can safely go is the next room over. Second, whatever excuse Loki comes up with to explain whatever he did to me, it's not like I can leave him.

Except… maybe I can.

Okay. *Okay.* He might have a perfectly decent explanation. He's been good to me, too. The least I can do is hear him out.

Deep breath, Kennedy.

In. Out.

Whoosa.

"Okay. Let's start from the beginning. Can we do that, Loki?"

His gaze flickers over to the bed. Though it's obvious he'd rather go back to doing what we were doing before, he nods. "Of course."

Right. "What did you do to me?"

Easy enough question.

He offers me an easy enough answer.

"I gave you my essence."

What is *that* supposed to mean?

"I know you must be surprised," Loki adds. "I am, too. I never thought I would be able to share it with you, but I did somehow."

Funny. I'm pretty sure I got plenty of 'essence' the first time I slept with him…

I shake my head. Unfortunately, that has the side effect of my naked boobs bouncing. As serious as I am right now, it only sets me off further when Loki's gaze dips down to watch them move.

Men. Demon or human, it doesn't matter, huh?

I snap my fingers, catching his attention.

"Ken-dee…" At my sharp look, he tries again. "Kennedy."

Better. "You're gonna explain this all to me, Loki. I'm gonna try my best to listen. But, first, I want you to give me my dress back."

Inside of my chest, I sense a wave of disappointment that I know sure as hell didn't come from me.

Seriously? Now I can add being able to feel his emotions to the list of how much I've changed because I decided to sleep with him for real?

This time, there's no 'dream' excuse. I wanted to feel him inside of me, and up until he orgasmed and suddenly I spoke Sombran, I was definitely into it.

Not right now.

Once I'm covered, I wave at him. "And you." A minute ago, his dick was inside of me. Shiny from fucking me and still hard as stone, I can't stand that thing winking at me while I'm trying to make sense of all this.

He nods. With another gesture, he weaves thick, dark shadows around his legs. It keeps going until it reaches his navel, leaving his sculpted chest bared.

Welp. Better than nothing.

As the shadows wound around him, Loki broke the silence with a question of his own.

"When you mentioned my eyes before, what did you mean?"

I'm sorry, but this is so freaking weird. I hear him making those guttural sounds I'm familiar with so I know he's speaking his demon language. Sombran. But when it hits my brain, it's like I instantly translate it into English.

His eyes? What—

Oh.

"They're purple now."

It was such a shock to me before. Coming down from facing off against that shadow beast, I did a double-take when I noticed that Loki's eyes went from purple to white. I got distracted after that... but there's no denying it. His eyes are definitely different.

"Ah. That would explain it."

For him, maybe. Me?

I'm still super fucking confused.

You know what, though? Forget it. I changed my mind. When he first brought me to Sombra, I spent those early days with Loki hoping that I would be able to talk to him and tell him I want to go back to my apartment.

Looks like now I can.

"Whatever. It doesn't matter what you did. You did it and now I can finally tell you that I want to go home."

His purple eyes brighten, going almost violet. Or

maybe that's a hint of the old white glow breaking through…

"What do you mean?"

"You heard me. I know you can understand me. That portal thing that we jumped in to get here? Make one. Bring me back."

Loki shakes his head. "I cannot do that."

Oh, yes, he can. "It wasn't my choice to come here. You have to admit that. I can't stay."

I would have. When I thought there was no other choice. But it's not just his language I suddenly know now. I also know that the spell I read all those weeks ago *was* magic. It summoned Loki from Sombra, depositing him in my world because *I* manifested him, and after he… he *seduced* me in what I thought was a dream, he opened the portal himself to bring us both back to his world.

I already knew that's what happened. I was there, right? What I didn't know, though? It wasn't an impulsive decision. He didn't stumble into a human's bedroom and think, gee, I wonder if I can have sex with her?

From the moment he arrived on Earth, he had every intention of bonding me to him. Of keeping me forever—and he did that with one look. *One* look was all it took. Our eyes met, the bond snapped into place, and even if I didn't think I was dreaming, that pull toward him would have been irresistible.

And, boy, I hadn't wanted to resist at all. Just like he doesn't want to let me go.

"Of course you can," Loki rumbles. "This is my home."

"Exactly. This is your world, not mine."

He frowns, the slight bumps over his nose scrunching together as his brow furrows.

"I said that wrong. This is *our* home. You are my mate."

His *what*?

Uxor mi… that's what he said. It translated instantly in my head—my *mate*—and I guess I finally have confirmation. All along I thought 'uxor' meant 'fuck'.

I was waaaaay off.

Even better, Loki says 'mate' and as though he explains the concept without words, I know instantly that Sombra demons spend their entire lives searching for their one true mate. Their one true love. When they find them, they claim them and bond them together, sharing their life and their—

Essence.

It happened again. Like I'm plugged right into his brain, I know things he does. Things I shouldn't.

What did he do to me?

"I thought your—"

"Essence," supplies Loki.

"Right. I thought that that just made it so that we

can speak to each other in Sombran. But that's not at all, is it?"

"I gave you everything I am."

I really have to yank my head out of the gutter. When Loki said he gave me his 'essence', I just thought that was demon speak for his jizz. It's not. A closer translation in English would be 'soul'.

Because he's my soul mate.

No. He's my *true love*.

Or he thinks he is. It's why he stole me. It's why he bends over backward to give me everything he thinks I need. Why he feeds me. Helps me wash my hair. Curls up into bed next to me to share his warmth.

It's why he's constantly aroused around me. I'm not just any woman.

I'm his.

As though he knows what I'm thinking—and who knows, maybe he *does*—he insists again, "You are my mate."

And Loki is convinced that his mate must live with him. He will never, ever take me home.

When that realization hits me, I have to admit to myself that I never really expected him to. Not after I'd spent a couple of days with Loki, not after these last couple of weeks, and especially not after I can get the chance to reach inside of him and find out what makes him tick.

I'm bonded to the beast, and whether he seems a

lot less beastlike now that I can understand him, it doesn't matter.

Somehow that makes it *worse*.

"I think I liked you better when I couldn't understand you," I snap at him.

"Kennedy—"

I can't go outside. We both know it's not safe for me. But Loki... he goes out there all the time to hunt. He took down that arkoda thing without breaking a sweat.

I point through the open door, gesturing at the closed one that leads outside. "Go away, Loki."

"Is that what you want?"

I want some space. "Yes."

He takes a deep breath. Shudders it out. "I will do anything for you. I want you to know that."

I do, and that's what makes this so freaking confusing.

Without another word, Loki starts for the door. When he reaches it, he tosses one glance over his shoulder, takes a deep breath, and shoves it open.

One step. That's all it takes. One step outside and Loki goes up in flames like a fireball. So used to the dark shadows, the red and orange flames tipped with white are blinding. It's excruciating, but knowing that fireball was Loki a split second ago is a million times worse.

I can't look away. In a panic, I rub my eyes quickly with the heels of my hands, desperate to get some of my vision back. Hoping that, when I do, it'll have all been a trick… or a mirage… something.

I squint.

He's still burning.

Oh my God. Oh my *God.* I told him to go and I *killed* him.

"Loki." Tears spring to my eyes as I take a few frantic steps toward him. Not because my eyes are in agony—which they are—but because the idea of losing my demon even if I'm pissed at him is too fucking much to bear. "Loki, *no!*"

"Shhh." As fast as he went up in flames, he's back. The room smells like rotten eggs and burnt hair, but when he meets me in the bathroom, he looks perfectly unharmed.

I'm glad it stinks. If it didn't, I'd think I'd imagined that. The lingering heat and the rotten air are all that's left of the fire.

Now that I see he's okay, I start to fume again. How could I have forgotten?

He can wield fire. He uses it to cook hunks of meat for me. His essence whispers the word 'mage' in my brain. Before he came to live in the shadows, he could do magic. It's slowly been coming back to him… how do I know that that wasn't a trick?

"Did you do that on purpose?" I demand.

"You leak."

I shouldn't laugh. This is the wrong time to laugh,

but I do anyway if only out of relief that, trick or not, he's okay. "It's called crying, Loki."

He nods sagely. "Of course. It's more human magic."

Only one of us can do magic here and it's him.

"How did you do that?"

"It wasn't me, my mate. The fire consumed me because of you."

"No, it didn't."

Yes, it did.

I already know the answer thanks to whatever exactly his essence did to me, but so stunned at the revelation, I stay quiet as he explains.

"We have a mate bond. I've given you my essence. Until you share yours with me, that will happen anytime you go too far from me."

And that's not all.

There's something called mate sickness. He'll burn if I don't give him my essence back and promise to be his bonded mate. Me? I'll suffer from a burning fever and need to fuck him until I do.

You have *got* to be kidding me.

"Did you know this would happen?"

"I never intended it to."

That's not a 'no'.

Damn it. I can't go outside because the same thing will happen if I stretch the length of the bond too far. As annoyed as I am, I can't stand watching him burn. Even though he's not harmed now, I'm pretty sure the agony I felt when my eyes were burning had an echo of Loki's pain to it. His shadowy form healed any injuries before he turned to demon, but it still hurt.

I exhale roughly and walk over to the bed. Plopping down on the edge, I ask, "And there's no way to reverse it?"

"You would ask that of me?"

That's not a 'no', either?

KENNEDY

This time, I sigh. "Loki…"

He comes over to me. Before I can say anything else, Loki drops to his knees, laying his head on my hip. He's careful to angle his head so that his horns are on either side of me.

"For four hundred years, I've dreamed of you. The other half of my soul. My one true mate. The female who would save me from the shadows."

My fingers ghost over his wild hair. I smelled it burn, but it seems alright. "That's a lot to ask of a woman, Loki."

"The gods wouldn't have given you to me if you could not."

"Is that what you think happened?"

"Of course. Why else would you have chanced on the grimoire with the matefinder spell and be able to cast it? You did what I could not, and I'll be grateful for the gift for every single day of our lives."

He sounds like I'm a done deal. With a sentiment like that... who knows? I might be.

"I waited for you." A harsh chuckle fans warm breath against my thigh. "Not very patiently at times, but in the shadows, I learned patience. Then your magic called me to you. I've given you my essence and my mate's promise. I'll be a good male to you. I vow it."

There's just enough solemn certainty in his tone that I know for sure that Loki... he really won't take me back. I could cry or 'leak' or even beg, and while he'll regret hurting me, this is the one thing he won't give me.

And I can't leave him.

I mean, I wouldn't. I might have stormed off because I need my space, but that's what I do. I throw shoes and I put distance between me and whatever pissed me off to the point that I felt the need to throw shoes in the first place. Then I think it through and make my decisions quickly.

It's usually easy. I saw Tyler cheating on me with my sister? Fine. I got away from them, and once I processed what I saw, I dumped his ass and cut her off. My parents, too, when they sided with the cheaters.

When it comes to Loki, it's just as easy.

The fury has died down. It's time to make my decision—and who am I kidding? I made it the same night that Loki let me keep Freya as a pet even though I'm pretty sure he still doesn't quite understand why I don't just eat her.

Besides, what would I really be going back for? Stuff? My store? There are books here in Sombra; I know, I have one. I can get more. Somehow.

And when it comes to a partner... do I want a human husband who might go looking for another lover when I don't pay him enough attention? Or a demon mate who wanted me so much, he stole me away with him so he can keep me?

"Okay. You got me." At the very least, I never want to see him go up in flames again. "What do I have to do?"

"Do?"

"Yeah. You said something about a bond and a mate's promise, right? So that I can avoid the mate sickness and you don't have to be a walking pyre. Tell me. How do I do that?"

"Kennedy... I thought—"

Yeah. I know what he probably thought. But while I might have his essence, now that we're communicating, Loki is getting to see another side of me. And this Kennedy? She reserves the right to change her mind quickly if she wants to.

He gives his head a clearing shake. "Do you love me?"

What?

Does it matter? I gave in. I said I would stay. That I would promise myself to him.

"I love you, my heart. Do you love me?"

When I don't answer, he holds out his hand. "Will you gift me your essence?"

He gave me his. That's what started this whole thing. And if I give him mine, he'll know everything about me. Growing up as the black sheep of my family with my golden child younger sister. Lonely days at high school, and mistakes I can't take back. Tyler. He'll know all of it.

And I'm almost positive it won't change a thing about the way he feels for me.

He called me his 'heart', after all. And from the emotions passing over to me when he says it, he's been thinking of me with that nickname for a while now.

But how am I supposed to give him my essence?

With a huff, I admit, "I don't know how."

"Put your wee hand in mine, my Kennedy. And just let me have it."

Don't tempt me, Loki. Right now, I kind of really want to let you have it… but probably not the way he means.

"Fine." I drop my hand into his. "Happy?"

His purple eyes gleam as anther spark passes

between us. He folds his red fingers over my pale hand.

"Yes," he says, his voice impossibly low. "I am very happy. Because I have your essence now and I can sense your feelings for me." Loki beams. "And you love me. Maybe not as much as I adore you, but that's only fair. I've longed for you my whole life, loving you in an instant. It will take more time for you to share my feelings, but I promise you, I will stop at nothing until you do."

I believe him. Is that crazy? It might be.

But if it is, it's no crazier than throwing away any hope of going back home ever again.

Ah, well. The human world is overrated.

What's a little thing like delivery at the push of a button, an apartment with an actual shower, and hundreds of books available on a device that's small enough to fit in my purse when I'm looking at true love?

Strangely enough, I actually mean that.

Because when Loki says my essence tells him I love him, I have to admit to myself: Huh. I guess I do.

"Essence, check," I tell him, trying not to grow red as he marvels down at me. I can only imagine what part of me or my memories—the very essence of who I am—he's tapping into right now to give him that look on his face... but I like it. "What's the mate's promise."

"It's a promise bonded mates say to each other when they choose one another."

Oh. Okay. Like wedding vows.

"If you want, you can repeat after me, my mate."

Will I ever not shiver when Loki says that in his gruff, rough voice? Probably not. "Okay."

"My soul will be yours—"

I open my mouth to repeat the first line of the promise when it hits me that I *know* this. And not because Loki does, either. I know it because I've heard that exact phrase before.

No. Not *heard* it. *Read* it.

At this point, I've probably read it a hundred times in Sombran, not having any idea what the strange words meant, but now that Loki says it out loud and I hear it in English, it hits me that the second part of the true love spell really *is* a promise.

I hold up one finger. "Hang on, okay? I want to see something."

As Loki watches me curiously, I get up from the bed and go over to where I left the grimoire.

As if it just belongs there, I've kept The Beanery receipt as a place marker on the page that changed my life. Flipping open to the true love spell, I bring the book over to the nearest floating light.

Tracing my fingertip down the page, I get to the first line of the passage marked 'promise'. I read it to myself first, and when it all makes sense to me for the first time ever, I read it out loud:

"My soul will be yours. My heart is in your hands. Our lives will be forever intertwined. I give myself to you. I give you everything."

That done, feeling no different than I did a second ago, I flip the book closed.

"Okay. What do we do now?"

White eyes or purple eyes, it doesn't matter. When Loki turns his high beams on me like that, I know exactly what we're going to do even before he disappears my shadowy dress.

Well. What did I expect?

We are mates, aren't we?

AS THOUGH EAGER TO PROVE THAT WE WERE FULLY bonded, Loki mated me into damn near unconsciousness. I finally had to push him off of me to get some sleep, grumbling as he laughed boyishly at how I used the same words from before, just in a whole different mood.

Now he knows that he's welcome, that I'm not going to leave him. That, plus the three different rounds of sex we had before I was kaput has him in such a good mood, it's almost contagious.

I don't know how long I slept for. Well-pleasured and pressed up against Loki's chest, when I finally wake up again, he's staring down at me.

"Morning, my mate."

It's funny how, in a world that's full of shadows, my body eventually found its own circadian rhythm. You'd think it was midnight if you looked out of the window, but when Loki says 'morning', I one hundred percent agree that it has to be.

"Mornin'."

"Would it make you happy if we returned to the village?"

Huh?

Okay. I'm not awake enough for an actual conversation, especially not one that catches me off guard. Times like these I miss my morning coffee, but since all Loki has is water, I had to give that up cold turkey.

More proof that my mate must really love me. That caffeine withdrawal was no joke, and if he could put up with me during those days when I was going through it, he'll put up with anything.

I blink the last of the sleep from my eyes and say, "What?"

He nuzzles the top of my head with his chin before pulling back. "While you were sleeping, I tried to think what I could do to make you happy. You want to go home."

I did. "Loki… I mated you. We're bonded. This is my home now. Our home."

He grins, showing me his fangs. I can sense his pleasure at hearing me say 'our', as well as his body stirring at the reminder of our mating.

However, instead of rolling me onto my back, he

stays on his side. "It is. But before I… lost myself to my shadows, I conjured another home for me and my future mate. Back in Nuit."

I've heard of that place before. No. Wait. That's a Loki thought. He knows Nuit, which means I do now.

It's the demon village that Loki used to live in before—

Ouch.

I thought I was over the worst of the withdrawal, but the sudden throbbing in my skull *hurt*.

"Kennedy?" Worry fills his tone. "You alright, my mate?"

I don't nod, just in case. "Yeah. Sorry. You were saying?"

"I was wondering if you wanted to come live with me in Nuit?"

Right. "Where you're from?"

"Where I was from before," Loki agrees. "Now that you've accepted me as yours, I thought… it's finer than this shack. I have many rooms. We would have neighbors." He pauses. From the way his eyes glimmer, I'm betting he's using my essence to see what would sway me. "It has a tub with warm water."

You know, one of these days I'm going to have to figure out how to tap into his essence and find out what led him to exile himself to the dark shadows with nothing but beasts for company. I'm not a pro at using his essence yet, so he's doing better than me, but it doesn't matter.

I'll go where he goes, and if I have to spend an eternity to learn what makes Loki *Loki*, I will.

Grinning at him, I lay my hand on his chest. "Put like that, how can a girl refuse?"

Honestly? He had me at tub.

CHAPTER 14
NUIT

KENNEDY

My mate wastes no time. After extinguishing the light spells in both rooms, he makes sure that I have Freya snuggled close before he lifts me up. At my urging, he grabs the *Grimoire du Sombra*, too, tucking it under his arm.

I leave my old dress behind.

Loki doesn't put me down again until we break free of the shadows. Surprisingly, it wasn't a very far walk. A little frightening since I kept expecting another one of those monster beasts to jump out at us, but as though the predators in the dark knew not to mess with Loki, they watched us with their bright white eyes, but kept their distance.

Walking out of the shadows is like willingly

walking into an oven. That's what the blast of dry air slamming into my face feels like.

The ground is weird, too. It was firmer in the dark. Out here, it's thick with a little give to it. Red flecked with grey, black, and white, it looks like someone took an ashtray and sprinkled it over a pile of paprika.

The sky is red, too. So is the moon hanging over my head.

It was black in the shadows, I think, before I have to say something about the heat.

"Holy shit, it's hot." I fan my face. "Were we in a refrigerator back there?"

Because, seriously, it's like a thirty-degree difference between the shadows and the heat—and that's with our temperatures matching now that we're fully bonded mates.

"Refrigerator?" Loki echoes.

Right. I forgot. Not every word in English has a direct translation. They obviously don't have anything like a fridge here.

Considering it's as hot as hell on the other side of the shadows, that makes sense. While there's magic in Sombra—the same kind of magic that makes it so Loki can conjure those light orbs of his—there's no electricity. Can you imagine if there was? How much energy would it take to keep anything cool in this hell world?

"Never mind."

I wave my hand and reach up to make sure that Freya is doing okay. With her shadowy fur, I don't know how she'll react to the heat, but considering she's just chittering away, it doesn't seem to bother her. She's probably just glad to be out of the shadows without an arkoda chasing her into a tree.

Glancing further, I see a whole bunch of structures spread out in the distance. They look more like small ranch houses, squat and flat but wide, and all of them are dark so it's hard to pick up too many details.

Following the direction of my stare, Loki says, "That is Nuit. Are you ready, my mate?"

Ready as I'm ever going to be. "Sure. Might sweat to death, but I'll be fine."

"To death?" murmurs my mate. "You are immortal now."

He's right. Another perk of his essence and our bond. I'll live as long as he does, and since he's immortal, so am I. Honestly, I'm still trying to come to grip with *that* one, and I've decided—at this point —to simple take everything one day at a time for now.

"Just an expression, Loki." I pat him on the arm. "Just an expression."

THERE'S NO REFRIGERATORS. NO PHONES, EITHER. NO way to give the leader of the village I'm dragging my feet through the ash toward any heads up that we're on the way.

And yet, just as we cross from the open space to the first line of demon houses, we're met by two villagers.

One of them is a Sombra demon male. He has the same red skin as Loki, though his horns are curved further back and he only has one pair. His eyes are different, too. A bright gold color gleams out of his cautious face as he approaches us.

The female at his side is nothing like the males. Her skin is as golden as the male's eyes, her orange hair is a long plait tossed over her shoulder. She's as tall as he is, though her deep brown horns are so dainty, they're adorable.

For a moment, I think that Sombra demon males look like Loki and this other guy, while their women look like this female, but a name pops right into my brain. *Soleil.* The neighboring demon realm where many Sombra males find their demoness mates.

She is a Soleil demoness, and obviously the other male's mate.

"Apollyon." Loki's brow furrows as though he's struggling to place her. He does. "Lilith."

"Loki?" The pretty demoness doesn't hide her surprise very well. "Can that really be you?" She glances at me, her amber-colored eyes going wide when she notices Freya curled around my neck… or maybe it's her shock at getting her first look at me. "Is that an ungez wrapped around this female's throat?"

Oh. It *was* Freya.

Loki lays his hand on my shoulder. "Yes, and yes. We've come to ask permission to join your clan. The three of us."

I beam.

Loki knows to include Freya, too.

The male demon frowns, and since he hasn't taken his attention off of Loki yet, I don't think that has to be because of my pet.

"You walked into the shadows," he says after a moment.

I was right.

Loki nods sharply. "I did."

"You were lost."

His Adam's apple bobs as he swallows roughly. "I was."

"No one survives the shadows," offers the demoness.

"No one except Loki," my mate says. "And all because of my Kennedy."

Loki believes that to the depths of his soul. He believes that he was lost and broken before he found me, and that I'm the reason why he has his purple eyes and his magic back.

"And you want to rejoin Nuit? I know we are not your birth clan. You came to us from Marvo. Not many choose a poorer village on the edge of the shadows."

Maybe not, but they probably aren't leaving the shadows, either.

He squeezes my shoulder, the points of his claws gone shadowy so that he doesn't prick me with them. "I have, Apollyon. If you will have us."

"You became a clansman when you came to Nuit and built your home here. It still stands." Apollyon holds out his hand. When Loki takes it with his free one, the golden-eyed demon pulls him into an embrace, clapping him on the back before releasing him. "Welcome home."

"And my Kennedy? I go where she goes. If she's not welcome, we will search for a new clan."

He explained this to me in hushed tones as we traveled to the demon village. Sombra might be ruled by its duke leader, Haures, but each individual neighborhood—er, clan—is run under one leader. For us to live among the villagers, we both need his welcome.

It's some weird demon respect thing. By welcoming us, Apollyon is giving us his protection. He will stand up for us against any threat, even shield us from the duke if he has to. But it works both ways. We need to listen to him and do what's best for the clan.

That's why Loki left Nuit. For some reason, he was a threat to it when his eyes were white, but now that his eyes are purple again, he can return home.

It's safer living in a community. Even in the

human world, we know there's safety in numbers. The monsters that lurk in the shadows by Loki's old shack would never enter Nuit.

I suck in a breath. He has a house here. He obviously knows these people. I hope they let me stay because I really, really don't want to go back to the dark shadows again.

"She is your bonded mate?"

Loki sticks out his chin. "Yes."

For some strange reason, the other demon's golden gaze dips to Loki's bare chest. Ever since I mentioned that, while I like his cock very much, I wouldn't mind if he kept it covered when we weren't mating, Loki wears shadows around his lower half. He's not as fully covered as Apollyon, but he's decent.

"Then she is clan as well. Welcome," he says. "Now, come. I will lead you to your home. It waits for you."

Home. Sombra isn't my home, not really, but it will be.

I bump Loki's side. "I can't wait."

OUR FIRST FEW DAYS IN THE VILLAGE GO BY QUICKLY mainly because there's so much for us to do.

The house that Loki built for his mate ages ago is much larger than his shack in the shadows. Four rooms instead of two, it has things much closer to what I was used to on Earth. Take the bathroom area. Instead of just a hole in the ground and a single water tube, he has an elaborate basin that can hold water in it, and a black glass covering the hole that reminds me of an actual toilet.

Like he promised me, there's the nicest bathtub I've ever seen, complete with its own water tube. Since Sombra is a hellish realm—literally—all of the water in the bathroom is the perfect temperature to soak. Plus, it's big enough to fit both Loki in his demon form and me comfortably.

I *love* it.

In the designated bedroom, he has a bed similar to the one in the shadows. More light, too, and windows. Above, there are circles built into the ceiling that let the moonlight shine down on us when we're snuggling.

He looks surprised when I point them out. That happens a lot when I ask about something that he thinks of as normal. Part of the essence exchange is making it so that mates know each other so intimately, there's no doubt they're made for each other. With his thoughts and memories passed over to me, I should know what they mean.

I don't, mainly because I try not to rely on Loki's essence. Something happened to him. Something that splintered this male, creating so many facets that he can be the seductive lover, the devoted mate, the fierce hunter, the intelligent mage, and the possessive beast all at the same time.

Too bad I don't know *what*.

Digging into his memories gives me a headache anytime I try. It's like there's a dark shadow covering almost everything he's ever known or experienced, and if I peek under it, we'll both hurt for it.

Besides, I'm human. Getting to know my lover— my mate—on my own is part of the fun. I'll take the download of his demon language gladly so that I can communicate with him. Everything else? If I want to know, I'll ask. Even if he thinks I *should* know, he answers anyway.

It works for us, and that's how I discover that Loki isn't just inhumanly fast. Those circles in the ceiling? Loki can turn to mist, so faded he's nearly invisible, before compressing and shooting right through that hole.

He can freaking *fly*.

It's shadow travel, he explains, and while it's not as quick as using a portal, it's common for Sombra demons to flit around like eddies of wind.

He's right. Every time I peek out of the window, I see at least one slightly dark shadow soaring overhead.

And that's not all. Every time I peek out of the window, I see another demon watching our house with interest.

I don't know who the bigger draw is: me or Loki.

I'm a human. I highly doubt that any of the residents on this demon plane has ever met someone like me before. I finally got the chance to ask Loki about the skull that scared the crap out of me when we first appeared in his old shack. I'm glad to hear that he found it just like it was, polished and clean and thrown in a pile of skulls in an old arkoda den. Something about it called to him, so he grabbed it and took it home with him.

In his own sweet way, he must have always known he was meant to mate a human woman. But the skull itself tells me that I probably wasn't the first human to visit this part of Sombra.

From the attention the villagers give me, you never would've known.

They think I look funny. I couldn't even blame the demon child—spawn, Loki told me, because the demons fittingly call their kids *spawn*—for the way he blurted out, "Mama, what is *that*?" when he first saw me. Even if he didn't, I've caught a glimpse of what Loki thought when he first saw me.

Colorless. No horns. No protective ridges. My ears are round instead of pointed, and my eyes are dim. To Loki, I was puny, my hair strangely soft, and yet… in a heartbeat, he decided that I was different, but I was his, and he learned to appreciate our differences.

Just like I did.

But if they think I'm weird, they're all interested in Loki. From what I understand, there was a reason the only creatures we found in the shadows were more like animals than people. It's rare to survive in there, and while I get a headache whenever I search Loki's essence to see why he existed so long in the dark, the villagers are as amazed as Apollyon that Loki returned to Nuit.

A hundred years. He spent *a hundred years* in that shack. That shouldn't shock me as much as it does. His essence tells me that he's closer to four hundred, but to other demons, he's still young.

Apollyon is over *a thousand*.

I like him. The clan leader is careful to warn the other villagers away while we're settling in. And when they don't listen to him? They definitely listen to the clanmother…

Now, I've never been shy. While it might seem like I'm avoiding being gawked at by the other demons, I decide to spend my first few days in the house because it needs dusting, airing out, and as much decorating as Loki's conjuring skills can give me. Now that he has more control over his magic, there isn't anything he can't create for me with the proper instruction… and motivation.

I ask for a couch. I get a couch.

We fuck on the couch.

I ask for shadow blankets. Now that we're bonded mates, my temperature matches his—just like my lifespan does—but I've always been a crea-ture of comfort. I want a blanket. He makes me countless.

Every single one of them ends up on the floor after another vigorous mating session.

Loki assures me that the lust I'm feeling is perfectly normal. It's our reward for becoming forever mates. He believes it's a blessing from the demon gods he reveres—that he thanks daily for giving me to him —and instead of suffering from mate sickness, we're both just horny as hell.

I've never had a guy so insatiable for me before. While it's tough for me to tap into Loki's essence and wade through his memories, I know enough that this is also completely normal for demon males. They wait their whole lives, no matter how long it takes, to find their fated female. I was his first, his last, his only.

And now that he has me, he wants to have me every way he can—and I'm okay with that.

Because while Loki wasn't my first or my only, he's the one I chose and I'm growing more and more confident in my decision every day.

Just like I'm falling more and more in love with my demon at the same time.

He makes it so easy. Especially when I can sense his love for me like a warmth in the center of my chest, pulsing down our bond… he means it when he tells me he loves me. I might have thought this was all about sex for him, but it isn't. Not entirely. Mating just reinforces our bond, while the little things he does for me day to day prove how much he cares.

Take my new dresses for example.

So used to weaving clothes out of shadows, Loki finds it frustratingly hard to create dresses and shorts and underwear out of fabric. I know someone can. The few glimpses of the female demons—demonesses—I got showed most of them wearing fabric clothes. Loki promises to get them for me, and by our second day here, I have one.

It's huge on me, obviously made for a demoness, but I'm so pleased with his effort to get one that I shrug it right off and basically jump my mate; well, after I made sure he didn't steal it. Demons see things differently than humans do—obviously, since Loki was convinced he had the right to take me with him when he recognized me as his mate—and I didn't want some demoness blaming him when one of her red dresses went missing.

He vows that he bartered for it. I believe him.

If there's one thing I'm certain of, it's that my demon mate will never, ever lie to me.

The other villagers are leery of him at first. Before long, though, they see how awesome it can be to have a mage around. When the only demon I knew was Loki, I figured everyone could do what he does.

Nope. Creating those floating lights that kept his shack illuminated in the shadows is considered a special talent. Conjuring things from thin air, too. No one else in Nuit has the gift, mainly because any purple-eyed demon is sent to the capital in Sombra to study magic.

Loki did once. The School of Mages is a faint memory that I pick out of his essence, but like everything else about him, when I prod it further, all I get is a nasty headache and more questions about this interesting male.

He's a mage. He lived in the shadows. I check out every demon in Nuit once I feel comfortable enough to walk around the village square. Loki is the only one that has *two* sets of horns.

When I point that out to him, he nuzzles me close before rumbling softly, "A unique human female for the most powerful two-horn. The gods knew to pair us up."

Who knows?

Maybe they did.

CHAPTER 15
THE GOLD MOON

KENNEDY

There's a reason why Apollyon's mate, Lilith, is known as the clanmother.

About a week after me, Loki, and Freya traveled into the village, taking over Loki's old, empty house, she arrived at the door with a platter of freshly baked buns with a sticky, sweet syrup on top and a book.

"Loki mentioned that you were a bookseller," she said warmly, handing over the platter of delicious-looking buns. "He also said that you only have one right now since you accepted him as your mate. I thought you'd like another."

Taking the book next, nearly squealing with delight that I finally had something to read that wasn't the *Grimoire du Sombra*, I invited Lilith in to share a bun and meet Freya.

With a kind smile, she told me, "Of course."

And that's how I get my first friend in Sombra.

Even better, she's a treasure trove of information.

I might not be able to always get the answers I want about life in Sombra from Loki or his essence, but Lilith isn't only the clanmother. She's the clan teacher, and while she tends to the spawn in the village, she makes time for me when she can considering there's always someone who needs her.

In fact, she's the reason I discover why Apollyon scrutinized Loki's chest after he told the clan leader we were mated when she asks innocently when Loki will be visiting Trost, the clan tattooist.

In Sombra, it's a tradition for bonded males to carve their mate's name into their chest, setting the brand with a shiny silver ink. Beneath his shadow coverings, Apollyon has Lilith's name etched into his chest.

After our first gold moon spent together in our new home, Loki will have mine.

Sombra has two moons. The darker, constant one is like the sun, only with less illumination and it never sets. The other is the gold moon, similar to the one in the human world in that it's not always there.

The gold moon is an event in Sombra. That's something else I learn. Matings are celebrated in the days leading up to it, any new spawn are introduced to the clan, and any demon who is ready to move on to another village says their goodbyes during the gold moon.

Plus, it makes bonded mates really, really horny.

As returning villagers, there's a feast in our honor on the night of our first gold moon together. No ungez, at Loki's thoughtful request, though it's definitely meat-heavy; a Sombran demon's preferred diet, I know now. There are still plenty of veggie dishes to round it out, enough to almost distract me from the flush turning my cheeks almost as red as Loki's, and the heat burning me inside out.

Almost.

I make it halfway through the second course before I find myself squirming in my seat, in need of my mate. Next to me, Loki is gripping the long table where we're sitting in the village square. His red knuckles are white from the pressure, his nostrils flaring as he breathes in the scent of my arousal.

We leave before the third course of meat is served or Lilith's deserts are brought out for the village, and though the feast was Nuit's way to welcome us, not a single demon stops us as we go.

Of course not. If they were once newly bonded to their forever mate, they know exactly what we are heading home to do.

I'M SO DESPERATE FOR LOKI, I DON'T EVEN MAKE IT to the bedroom.

Good thing I don't have to. With the billowy, black couch he conjured for us—because, when in doubt, Loki uses shadow to shape the things he sees through my essence—being big enough to fit the two of us comfortably, I wrap my fingers around two of his thick, knobby ones and tug him toward that.

"My Kennedy?" Loki's voice is so deep, I sense the vibration it makes more than I hear the words. "Are you feeling well, my heart?"

Feeling well? Depends on what he considers 'well'. Am I so horny that just the friction of my thighs rubbing together has me itching to shove my hand under my skirt? Oh, yes. But since we made it inside, the couch right there, I'll be okay as soon as I can get naked.

"I'm fine," I assure my concerned mate. Letting go of his fingers, I grab my dress by the hem. It's one of the ones he bartered doing magic for so, unlike the shadow outfits, I can take it off without his help. As I do, I tell him honestly, "Be better if we can mate."

"*Kennedy.*"

He sounds stunned.

Tossing my dress to the floor, I glance up at Loki. His eyes have darkened; instead of purple, they're a deep violet shade. His hands are twitching at his sides, the tips of his claws flicking through the edge of the shadow coverings wrapped around his meaty thighs.

I don't know why he's gazing down at my boobs like he's never seen them before. The rest of my naked body, either. I'm not shy. I was half-naked the night the true love spell summoned him to my bedroom, and even before I learned I was his fated mate, Loki caught glimpses of me during my quick sponge baths at the water tube in his shack.

Without being able to communicate, it wasn't worth the effort to kick him out of the toilet area when he was determined to watch over me, keeping me safe from anyone who might try to steal me away from him. Back then, I just thought he was being a bit of a perv, and I went ahead and washed up regardless if only to show him what he couldn't have.

Now? There are days when Loki conjures shadows to black out the windows in our home so the two of us can walk around naked. After a hundred years on his own, he prefers it, and it's pretty flattering to know that my mate thinks my naked body—blemishes, cellulite, stretch marks, rolls, and all—is the most beautiful thing he's ever seen in his long, immortal life.

We'd both gotten dressed to head to the village square for the feast. I'm quick to shuck off my dress. Loki? He lifts a trembling hand to his mouth, wiping the corner of his lips with the back of his massive mitt.

I give him my most innocent grin. "What's the matter, Loki? Got a little drool there?"

"I smell you, my mate," he growls softly in answer, his expression part-amazed, part-ravenous. "You smell *delicious*."

Yes on the drool, then. "Hungry?" I tease.

"We did leave the meal early."

He's lucky I lasted as long as I did. "Is that okay? We can go back if you want to."

Big as he is, he needs to eat a lot. Maybe we should have finished dinner even if the other villagers weren't surprised we cut out so early. According to Loki's essence and a few demure comments Lilith made, everyone knows that the gold moon acts like Spanish fly for Sombra demons.

Through our bond, I can tell that Loki is always ready to mate. It's not as desperate a need for him as it is me if only because he has, like, four centuries of celibacy to make up for.

But if he'd rather eat...

Loki doesn't answer me. Figuring he's still distracted by me, I start to bend over, reaching for my discarded dress—

"*Oh!*"

The fabric slips through my fingers as, all of a sudden, my equilibrium shifts. A red arm wraps around my middle, hefting me up, shifting and tilting me until he has one arm under my thighs, the other cradling my back.

I love it. I love *him*, but there's something about

the way he takes charge. Before I knew Loki, I thought it caveman-like. I called him a 'beast' when thinking of how he swung me around, eating me out in my closet before tossing me over his shoulder. Despite being sweet and devoted, my demon mate is still all of those things and he proves it when he starts marching away with me held tightly in his arms.

I tap his chest. "The couch," I tell him.

Loki detours, his jaw tight in concentration as he heads right for the shadow furniture.

He lays me out on the couch.

"I take it we're staying in," I say, stifling a giggle.

"You asked me if your mate is hungry. I am. I've hungered for a taste the entire moon."

Loki's in his demon form. His claws, however, are shadow so that he doesn't accidentally cut me as he reaches between my legs, dipping his finger past my folds. Taking his hand back, his shadow claw glistening with my cream, he slips it into his mouth.

After laving it clean with his tongue, his eyes flash brighter. "Ah, my Kennedy. A feast fit for this Sombra male."

Sombra is a hellish realm. I've gotten used to it since I've lived in Nuit with my mate, but when he looks at me like that? Heat rushes through me, pooling in my belly, amping my need up to eleven.

Loki starts to sink to the floor. I know what he's planning. Given the option, he will park his big demon body between my thighs and lick until I have to nudge his front horns with my heel to give him some sign that I'm ready for him to stop. And while, normally, I'm all for letting him worship me with his mouth—or for me to take my time, licking the purplish head of his cock like it's a damn lollipop, there's something about tonight.

I need *more*.

As his knees hit the floor, I notice something that has me struggling to sit up. Loki... he's still wearing his shadow covering. Whenever I initiate mating and he's dressed, he's naked even before I can think about taking off my dress.

He makes a small sound of disappointment in the back of his throat when I sit up, then go to my knees in front of him. No surprise. In this position, his mouth doesn't have the access to my pussy that he wanted.

I'm confused. I can sense him dying to mount me, to mate me... but it seems like he's just planning on giving me oral.

Honestly? That would be fine. I love oral. Tyler rarely went down on me, and I'd think Loki's fixation with my taste has something to do with one-upping my ex except for two reasons: one) Loki is confident enough in our bond that he only hates Tyler for hurting me, and two) he just really, really enjoys going down on me.

But he loves having sex with me, too. So why has

his demonic expression turned dark, his body thrumming with both need and nerves, almost as though he's not sure of his welcome?

Since our essence exchange and the mate's promise, I've always welcomed him. He should know that.

In case he doesn't, I'm going to make sure he does.

"Loki?" I ask. "If you don't want to mate tonight, that's fine, but I thought…"

"It's the gold moon, my mate," Loki answers. "Let me lick you 'til you cry my name. It'll help you with the need to mate."

"Or, and I'm just throwing it out there 'cause I'm naked and horny, but if you're feeling the need to mate, too, we can… you know… just mate."

Loki looks like that's all he wants. And, yet, he's still wearing those shadow coverings.

"Are you sure you're ready? This… this is something I've longed for… that I dreamed of for many cycles."

It all comes down to what the gold moon means. A sign of fertility, celebration, and joy to his people, it's like Easter, I guess. A celebration that comes once a cycle, with the side effect that it really gets bonded couples' libidos revving.

I want to show him that I will never doubt him. I might have once, but Kennedy goes all in. With her life, with her love, with her heart, she will give him everything he's ever wanted because he's given me everything I never knew I needed.

I open my arms to him. "I'm yours, Loki. We're bonded, right?"

"We are."

"And you want to mate me tonight, don't you?"

He swallows his groan. "The gods know I do, more than anything."

I grin at him, laying back down. My legs fall open, a temptation I know my demon won't be able to ignore. "So, come on."

Loki stands still for a moment, silent as a seven-foot-tall statue, carved of marble, painted red—until he shudders out a breath, the sense of sudden antici-pation prickling against my naked skin.

For the first time since I came to Nuit, I have chills as Loki waves one in front of his groin. His shadow coverings disappear, his eight-inch monster springing out to greet me.

When we first mated, Loki was an inexperienced virgin. He had the equipment to get the job done, but not the know-how to make it last. I didn't care. There were nights when he would go off within a few thrusts, sure. Considering it took a lot more than that for his cock to eventually go down—because, miracu-lously, he wasn't *always* hard around me... just most of the time—and Loki never stopped until I was writhing in pleasure beneath him, it didn't bother me that he couldn't last.

It's been a couple of weeks since our first mating. His stamina is definitely improving, and we've learned how to take our time with each other.

On the night of the gold moon, that's the last thing we do…

LOKI

THREE CYCLES LATER

I see a new side to my Kennedy in Nuit. Already the light to my shadows, she flourishes in the village.

The clansmen adore her. Not as much as I do, but though many treated her as other when I first brought her here, they quickly fell under her charms. There's something about her sweet smile and her blunt human teeth that make her seem so unthreatening. A demon's instincts would be to shield her as we would spawn.

My instincts are to do so much more than that

which is why my Kennedy is finally expecting our spawn.

It's still early. Only a few cycles have passed since I first sensed the new life growing inside of her. Her scent has barely changed. Recently, though, when I leave our home to barter for everything she would need, I get used to the knowing looks from my clansmen.

They do not mention it. Until the spawn is here and part of the village, it is our way to continue on as if our mates are not preparing for offspring. It will be a great celebration when my Kennedy gives birth. For now, it is all about pampering my mate and doing whatever I can to worship her as her amazing human body works hard to create our offspring.

She wants fabric-woven dresses? I trade Raiga a spell to keep her needles sharp for three new ones. A pair of boots made from the skin of a nadu, one of the leathery beasts who scamper through the ash fields in a brown-skinned solid form came from Del; all the elder demon required was to sit with Kennedy, learning secrets of her human world.

Lilith, Apollyon's mate, brings her books to read when she discovers that is my clever mate's specialty. Before she met me, my mate was a respected book-seller; it is how she found the spellbook that called me to her. In Nuit, Lilith acts as clanmother and teacher, so it is no wonder to me that the Soleil demoness takes my Kennedy under her horns.

I am glad that she is so welcomed by the villagers. From her essence, I know that my mate was lonely before she found me. I don't travel through her memories often. I learned my lesson when I learned of the male Tyler.

Humans do not mate for life like Sombra demons do. They can, and Kennedy assures me that some do, but it isn't expected. They trade mates frequently instead of waiting for their one true love. Of course. Demons have forever to find their mate, claim them, and keep them. Before my essence made Kennedy as immortal as any demoness, she only had a hundred years at most. With so little time, their people cannot risk waiting too long in the hopes they find their mate.

That's why she couldn't understand why I was so sure that she was mine. She felt the bond snap into place when I first walked into her human quarters, she just didn't know that's what it was. That she was meant to be mine until I could finally give her my essence.

She was meant to be mine, but she had other males before me.

Sombra demons are as possessive as we are protective. It wasn't rage I experienced because there was another. It was pain for how the worthless human male treated my precious Kennedy before I could save her from him.

She is my treasured mate. That she loved then was betrayed by another only hurts because it left a scar on her. Her ex-male was not worthy of her, but without him choosing another female over her—her kin, no less—would she ever have manifested me with magic of her own?

In a way, I thank the feckless human male. His loss is my gain, and I thank the gods every day for giving me another chance—and Kennedy.

She is my heart. My love. Everything I wanted, and nothing I deserved. When she curls up next to me on the 'couch' I conjured for her to her exact expectations, Freya sitting on her shoulder, another book from Lilith in her lap, I often marvel at my good fortune.

She saved me. I once thought of it as her healing me, but it's more than that.

I found my magic inside of my mate. I still struggle with my shadows—I probably always will, the aftereffects of the matefinder spell I cast so long ago—but where my well of magic ran dry the entire time I hid on the edge of Sombra, with my Kennedy at my side, it overflows.

And if anyone ever tries to take her from me, I will use my claws, my fangs, my two-horns, and my magic to stop them.

Cycles ago, I showed the arkoda mercy.

That is the last time I ever will if my Kennedy is threatened.

Cycles pass. In Sombra, we measure time by the rise and the fall of the gold moon. There have been three since the night Kennedy welcomed me with open arms and the spark of life that will one day be our spawn came to be.

Demonesses grow their offspring for twelve cycles. Her belly will go round somewhere around the eighth. It is customary to ignore the presence of the spawn until then.

Demonesses—and now my Kennedy—are more than just a vessel to a new soul. They are revered as the creators they are once the spawn shows signs of nearly arriving. Before then, it's about taking care of the mother, making sure she wants for nothing.

Today, Kennedy wants to go for a walk. 'Stretch her legs' as my mate puts it. A simple enough request, and wanting to please her, I ask if she wants to let Freya trot alongside us. Many of the villagers think it odd that my mate keeps a prey beast as a companion, but thanks to her essence, I know that Kennedy thinks of the ungez as her 'pet'. It reminds her of a domesticated animal from her world, and so long as she's happy in Sombra, I'll let her keep as many ungez as she likes.

Fortunately, she only desires the one. And since she dotes on the creature—pride wells up inside of me when I think of what a fine mother she'll be to our spawn—she asks it if it wants to join us.

Ungez don't speak. They chitter and chatter and

scratch our floor, but I've yet to hear one speak. Of course, my Kennedy insists she understands Freya.

More human magic, I once thought, before getting to truly know my mate. She is teasing, and it makes me adore her more for it.

According to her, Freya would rather curl up on the couch and sleep than stroll around the village square. Since that means I don't have to chase the ungez when it inevitably gets curious and runs off, I'm glad.

My good mood lasts throughout our stroll. In the cycles since we arrived in Nuit, the villagers have accepted Kennedy as one of their own, even though she is the only human many of the demons have ever seen.

At least, that's what I thought… until I hear someone call out Kennedy's name while we're walking together through the village square.

It's the way they say it. With her essence inside of me, I know precisely how my mate's odd human name is pronounced. The other demons? When they use her name, it sounds more like how I once said it: *Ken-dee*.

The pale-haired, white-skinned female shouting for my mate? She said "Kennedy" with a distinctly human accent.

I go still, predatory instincts at the fore even as my hands crackle with magic.

A human is here. It matters not that she has a

Sombra demon of her own shadowing her, or that Kennedy has not mentioned returning to the human world since long before the night of our first gold moon together.

I see the female and the dark shadows I've worked so hard to banish rise up suddenly. I shift from demon to my less substantial form, torn between running back to the edge of Sombra with Kennedy and challenging the human female and her mate for daring to come take *my* mate from me.

How else would they know her name unless, somehow, they came to return her to the human world?

I took her first. She's *mine*.

Kennedy's gaze slides my way. Bristling in place, torn between fighting and fleeing, she must sense my confusion—and my growing rage—through our bond.

"Loki? You okay?"

I will be.

I don't want to jostle Kennedy or our spawn so I decide not to grab her and run. Instead, digging my heels in the dirt, I lower my head so that my two-horns are ready to defend us against anyone who would take her from me.

"Loki? What are you doing? Are you feeling alright?"

"Kennedy!"

It hits me then that my mate's human hearing did

not pick up on the other female calling her name the first time.

Now that she has, she spins around, hair fanning behind her as a brilliant smile flashes across her face. "Shannon? Oh my God. *Shannon.*"

"I knew it," the pale-haired human female calls out in Kennedy's language. "I freaking knew it. This is where you've been all this time?"

"What are you doing here?" Kennedy's attention falls on the male demon. "Holy shit. You got one, too?"

"Yup," Shannon says proudly. "This is my mate. Malphas."

Malphas. I remember him now. Before I left for the shadows, he was the clan artist of Nuit.

Not a hunter, I think. Or a fighter. If I must battle him to keep my Kennedy, the odds are in my favor.

"Hold up, big guy." Shannon lifts up her hand, addressing me. "You look pretty pissed off there for some reason." Dropping it, she rests her palm on her belly. "I've got a baby on board, alright? Keep your distance."

"As does she, my mate," rumbles the artist before glancing up at me, his golden gaze fiercely protective as he moves in front of his female.

Shannon barely notices. Gaping at my mate, her eyes as strangely pale as her hair, she gasps, "Kennedy? You're pregnant, too? Awesome!"

"I— *what?*"

Through the bond, I sense my mate's surprise, followed quickly by the sensation that she is going to throw up her morning meal.

That is not good. For cycles, I've been encouraging her to eat enough; already so much smaller than a demoness, she cannot afford to lose her meal. I'd even bartered a renewing light spell for some of Moloch's stores of fresh meat. No ungez, at Kennedy's request, but the lean porrit—similar to something Kennedy enjoyed called 'chicken' in the human language—has enough nutrients to keep her strong while she's carrying our spawn.

Only that's the reason behind her sudden queasiness and her surprise.

My sweet mate didn't know she was expecting—at least, not until Malphas just told her she was.

And when she turns on me, her pretty human face creased in scrunched lines, I see that her eyes are watering.

She's leaking.

Something made my mate leak... no, *cry*... and sensing her upset, it's because of *me* that Kennedy cries.

I hurriedly straighten, no longer prepared to challenge the others. My attention is solely on my mate.

I don't understand what it is that I did, though it's clear the fault for her tears is mine. Even the bonded couple standing before us are aware of that.

When the pale-haired human makes a sympathetic sound, I want to tell her to leave us. I made her cry, but the female's unexpected appearance in Nuit has somehow affected my mate. She should go. This is our home. It might have been Malphas's once, but he was gone and I returned with my Kennedy.

My Kennedy...

Ignoring the others, I take a step toward her, my hand outstretched. She's frozen in place, the same sort of expression on her face that she wore when I first brought her to Sombra. Not quite fear or fury, but she's not gazing up at me with love and affection as she normally does.

She looks at me as if she doesn't know me.

I reach for her. She turns from me.

Suddenly, the scent of blood fills the air.

"Kennedy," I rumble, horrified that I cut her. It does not matter that she jerked her head away from me or that I never meant to harm her. I should have been more careful even so. "I didn't mean—"

Her tiny hand covers the edge of her jaw. "Don't worry about it. I just... is it true? Loki, am I pregnant?"

She's slipped into her Earth language. On purpose? I'm not so sure. Since I gave her my essence, we've mostly spoken Sombran to each other. In her eager way, she wanted to fit in with the rest of the village.

Her human language is something she uses when we're alone. Almost like it's a secret just between us.

I don't think that's what she is doing now. Eyes darting to and fro, her tiny human teeth nibbling her lush bottom lip, her mind is blank. I cannot tell how my human mate is feeling past the sudden surprise that flashed through her.

And it hits me: my Kennedy was unaware that she was with spawn.

"I... yes. For many cycles now." I step toward her. Her hand still covers her face. "Let me see. You are bleeding, my heart."

She doesn't move her hand. I reach to lay my palm on her fingers, to guide them away, but Kennedy jerks away from me.

My mate refuses my touch.

The old familiar ache starts low in my belly. "Kennedy?"

"I— don't touch me. Not right now. I... I have to think, okay."

"Don't touch you?" I echo. A muscle feathers in my jaw as I bite down, my fangs digging into my skin. A bloom of my blood joins Kennedy's. "You are my mate—"

Human eyes don't glow. When I first noticed that about my Kennedy, I was surprised, though I understood shortly after. It's a sign that a creature is immortal. Demons and demonic beasts have a never-ending life force until it's cut short, one way or another. By being hunted, or Duke Haures orders an execution, we only die when a powerful outside force lands a killing blow.

Not humans. They can die from so many things. It was a relief when I bonded her fully to me. She's my immortal mate now, though her eyes are still as dim and as dark and pretty as they were when we first met.

They don't glow, but like I discovered shortly after I brought Kennedy to Sombra—or, as she teasingly tells me, stole her away—they can flash angrily.

They are now.

"Yeah. I am. I remember that part. But you know what I don't remember? You telling me that I'm *pregnant*."

Why would I have? It's like telling her that the sky is red or the shadows are dark or I love her with everything I am. Some things just are, and Kennedy creating our offspring inside of her is one of them.

"Kennedy—"

She holds up her hand. Careful to keep the mark on her skin covered, she uses the other one to ward me off.

I freeze.

"Don't follow me, Loki," she snaps. "Not yet. I need to think. I need… just don't follow me."

And before I can do anything to calm her, she turns her back on me, leaving me behind.

CHAPTER 17
SURPRISE

KENNEDY

Despite what I said, I totally expect Loki to follow after me.

He's my shadow, right? That's what he does.

So when I hear steps right on my heels, I think it's him for about maybe three seconds before I realize that they're too light, and my innate awareness of where my mate is at all times tells me that he hasn't moved an inch since I stormed away from him.

Smart demon. I expected him to follow me, but as twisted up as I am right now, I don't know how I would react if he didn't give me some space. It's hard to explain, but in a way, it's like the shock of finding Tyler in bed with Hallie all over again only, this time,

I don't have a pair of heels to throw at him to vent my frustration.

Not that I would. I'm honestly shocked, but not exactly furious. At least, not how I was when I realized that two people I loved had betrayed me. Loki might have kept this little tidbit from me, but it's not like it's bad news.

It's not—and my happiness mingled with confusion with just a touch of hurt that I'm the last to know has me putting distance between us until I can figure out how exactly I should react to this new bombshell.

Pregnant.

The p-word.

Something I thought I gave up any chance of being when I promised myself to Loki. All I ever wanted was someone to love me, a family we could build together, and if that was just my mate and me, I was okay with that.

Kennedy adapts. Kennedy does what she has to to survive.

No kids? Fine. I got forever with Loki instead. A fair trade-off—or so I thought.

But *pregnant*?

Maybe it's my fault, too. Sure, he didn't tell me.

Me? I didn't ask.

I guess I just assumed that with him being a demon and me being human, we couldn't have kids. Looking back, I'm not so sure *why* I was convinced of that. If fate or Loki's gods or whatever made it so that we were meant for each other, why wouldn't we be able to have offspring of our own?

I just... I really thought we couldn't. So I tucked that little hope up and out of sight, never mentioning it to my mate in case it reminded him of something we couldn't have... and all along he knew we *could*. He *knew*, and he didn't say anything because he must have figured that—from his essence—I did, too.

Only I didn't, did I?

So, yeah... I'm not really mad at my mate. How can I be when he had no ill intentions?

But, then again, I've always been the type of woman who reacts first, thinking better about my actions after. Throw in some hormones from my newly-discovered pregnancy? I've gotta admit: storming away is a very Kennedy thing to do.

And I do it.

Marching up to our house, I fling open the front door, slamming it shut behind me once I step inside. My knees wobbly, I sink down on the nearest piece of furniture I can find. Freya's head jerks up as my ass hits the seat. As though she can sense my mood, she jumps down from her chair across the room, nuzzling my boot before joining me on mine. She scurries up to the top of my chair, her fluffy tail curling about the back of my neck as she steps onto my shoulder.

Absently, I reach up, stroking her fur. That helps.

My sweet little squirrel-cat, her soft chitters and her twitching whiskers… it helps a lot.

I shudder out a breath, already calming slightly.

A moment later, the door creaks open, Shannon's blonde head and cheeky smile peeking around the side of it.

Of course. That explains the lighter footsteps that had followed behind me.

"Can I come in?"

Five minutes ago, I would've been elated to see a fellow human. For it to be someone I actually know, I would've dragged her into the house so we could talk. So much about my last day on Earth makes sense once I realize that Shannon has her own Sombra demon mate. Her questions about the grimoire, the way she kept looking around the store… especially how I found The Beanery receipt marking the 'true love' spell that summoned Loki to me.

But that was five minutes ago.

Still, it was nice of her to come after me. And if she's also pregnant, she's probably the one person in either world who has any idea about the emotions tearing through me right now.

"Yeah," I say. "Go right ahead."

She slips into the house, easing the door closed behind her. I can see her glancing around, marveling at the home I share with Loki, gawking at Freya, though she gets herself focused by the time she's standing in front of me.

"So, uh, is this a 'congratulations' moment or should I start looking for something that could be used as a tissue?" Shannon starts patting the front pockets of her jeans, then the back. "I didn't bring my purse or anything since, well, *Sombra*, but here." Grabbing the edge of her sleeve, she yanks it down her forearm, stretching it out past her fingers.

Crouching low, she sticks it in my face. "Here. You need to wipe, use this."

I don't want to laugh. She sounds so earnest, and I'm on the edge of crying if only out of frustration, but as much as I don't want to laugh, I can't help it even as I tell her, "I'm good."

"That's a relief." Shannon rises up, shoving her sleeve back to her elbows. "Sorry, but it's fucking *hot* here. I should've listened to Mal and worn a tank top if I knew we were visiting his hometown a bit."

There's so much I want to ask her. I want to know about her mate—about this Mal—and how she mentioned Nuit being his hometown. Going even further back, I'm dying to find out what it's like with her mate. They obviously live back in the human world still, unlike me and Loki.

Like, what's that about?

But instead of all of that, I blurt out instead: "So… you're pregnant."

She doesn't look surprised by my comment—or taken aback by how bluntly I said that.

"Yup." She rubs her belly, as flat as I remember it

from the last time I saw her. "Got me a half-Shannon, half-Mal baby baking away inside of me. And you…" Her gaze dips to my lap. Yup. I don't look any different either, so I'm not surprised when she asks, "How far along are you?"

My next laugh is a hollow one. "Honestly? You tell me. It could go back to the day I met him. My first time with Loki, I was so… I don't know…"

"So distracted by shadow dick?" offers Shannon.

You could say that again.

"Something like that. Anyway, I never even thought about protection. Then, when we started being intimate more regularly, I figured it didn't matter. He's a demon. I'm human. It never occurred to me that we could get pregnant."

Shannon's eyes sparkle, reflecting the soft white light of the nearest magic orb. "Yeah. I thought the same thing, too. Then, surprise!"

Surprise is definitely the word for it.

"But I still get my period." I missed one month, but I thought that was the stress getting to me… and maybe it was. Having a half-demon baby might be different than a human one. "And look." I pat my lower belly. I have a pooch, but I don't look any different than I did months ago. "Loki's fucking *huge*. If my baby is part demon, shouldn't I have a big ol' baby bump by now?"

"From what I understand, you will. Eventually. It

just… even when a demoness is knocked up, it takes some time for her to show."

I don't know why, but something about the way Shannon says that has me going still. *Takes some time…*

"What about us? Human women?" I'm not rude enough to point out that she doesn't look like she's carrying any kind of demon baby, either. So unless she only just found out she is… "How far along are you?"

"Best guess?"

I nod.

"Just about a year."

"A year?" I squeal. "You've been pregnant for a *year*?" Wait a second. If she's been pregnant for a year and she's still waiting to show, then… "How long before the baby is here?"

"You want another guess?"

Honestly? I'm not so sure I do anymore. "Just tell me."

"Demonesses are pregnant for three years. Since we're half human, I'm hoping this baby gets the eviction notice somewhere around eighteen months or so, but I won't know until then."

My jaw drops.

Shannon nods. "Lucky me, right? I figure I got knocked up my first time with Mal even though I only just found out a couple of months ago myself." Shannon gives a two-finger salute to my ceiling. "Thanks for that, gold moon."

Gold moon? "What do you mean? What does the gold moon have to do with any of this?"

"Don't you have your mate's essence? I mean, you've gotta or else there wouldn't be a li'l Loki on the way." Shannon pauses, then cocks her head, her ponytail settling over her shoulder. "Really? That's his name? Not a nickname like I gave Mal?"

I nod. Loki's name—despite me having a similar reaction when I heard it—is the last thing on my mind right now.

Because Shannon's right. I *do* have Loki's essence.

True, I've learned it's better not to delve too deeply into his memories in case I see what it's like when he was lost in the shadows on the edge of Sombra; that only leads to headaches. Now that he's slowly becoming the male he was before he banished himself out there, his surface memories are fresh and new and full of love for me. I prefer those, and when I search them for any mention of the gold moon, all I get are flashes of the gold light splashed across my naked body as we mate... and another inexplicable pang that has me rubbing my temple.

Weird.

Shannon thinks so, too. "You okay, Kennedy?"

No. "I'm fine. And if Loki knows about the gold moon, it's not anything he passed on to me."

"I'm not surprised. I used to think of the essence swap like a download of Mal right into my brain. I know better now. If Mal thinks something is common knowledge, then it isn't important enough to imprint on his essence. Same for me. Even after a year with him, we're still having miscommunications here and there." Leaning forward, concern in her petty blue eyes even as a teasing look flashes across her face, she pats my knee. "Remind me to tell you about Mal's first Christmas with me and just what he thought a Santa Claws was."

I don't know Shannon all that well. She was a repeat customer who I ended up stealing from, whether I meant to or not. And while she's acting like we're old buddies, trying to comfort me in her own way, I'm barely listening to her right now.

Oh, no. I'm too hung up on something she said before—and the way my headache vanished as suddenly as it came.

And that's not all. The bond I have with Loki, the tie that tells me that he's on the other side always… it's suddenly dim, like he knows I'm struggling to process my emotions and he's giving me even more space.

Truth is, I can't sense him anymore. For the first time since our eyes met and our bond snapped into place, he's *gone*.

I almost get up to go to him, to make sure he's alright. Only Shannon's expectant expression and the way she kept saying 'year' like that has me staying in my seat, still stroking Freya's tail absently.

A year. She repeatedly mentions that it's been a

year since she mated her monster. I didn't correct her before because I'm trying to come to grips with the little surprise that I'm freaking *pregnant*, but I don't understand how she could be with her Sombra demon for a year now if it's only been six months or so since I sold her the grimoire.

But then she mentions Christmas and *that* catches my attention. Beneath her comforting pat, my whole body goes rigid—and not just because Loki's presence is an empty ache in my chest.

Christmas is in December. When I was in Jericho last, it was May. Add that to the fact that I'm the one who sold Shannon the *Grimoire du Sombra* in the first place and that was only… four months ago? I haven't really kept track of how many days have passed here in the demon world—I gave up shortly after we came to stay in Nuit—but I distinctly remember seeing four, maybe five gold moons rising up over the shadows.

In Nuit, it's always noticeable. The reddish-black moon is constantly out, the only source of light we have, but once a cycle, the gold moon begins to rise. It takes about three days from start to finish, and when it's at its highest, even the ash fields on the far side of Nuit glitter with the color. It doesn't do anything to quench the constant heat. In fact, when the gold moon is out, we all experience a different kind of heat.

And, suddenly, I think I know what Shannon is trying to tell me.

"The gold moon... is it some kind of aphrodisiac here in Sombra or something?"

"You could say that. Only it doesn't just affect the bonded couples who live on this plane. If they're on Earth like Mal and me, it does the same thing. Obviously," she adds, nodding her chin at her nonexistent belly. "And while it gets us going, that's only 'cause the whole point of these demons finding their one true mate is to start a family. You have sex on the night of the gold moon, it doesn't matter how good your birth control is. If you're bonded, you're as good as pregnant."

That doesn't make sense—and, wait a second, yes. Yes, it does. A certainty pops into my brain—this one courtesy of my mate's essence, still there though he's missing—and I know that, on the night of the gold moon, bonded couples tend to nuzzle and snuggle but don't actually fuck unless they want to add to their immediate clan.

That's something he *does* know. And he had every intention of reminding me during our first gold moon as bonded mates... but then he laid me out on our couch, discarding my dress and begging him to fuck me. He'd hesitated, offering to go down on me; because it was the gold moon, he just wanted to give me pleasure to slake our lust. But then I begged him to fill me, to fuck me, to mate me... and Loki took that to mean I wanted him to breed me.

Because I'm his mate, and I have his essence.

Everyone knows that rutting on the night of the gold moon guarantees spawn.

Everyone, it seems, except for Kennedy Barnes.

Shannon watches my face as I work to process all of my emotions. I've never been the type of woman to hide what I was feeling so I'm betting she got a full play-by-play of everything I was thinking as I thought it.

When she gives me a sympathetic smile and says, "Don't feel bad, Kennedy, I didn't realize it myself until it was too late," and I'm sure I'm right.

And then she adds, with a soft chuckle, "At least you didn't think something was seriously wrong with you before someone else's demon mate blurted out you were carrying your mate's spawn. The first time my hand turned to shadow… that so wasn't cool."

I blink. "Your human hand turned to shadow?"

"Oh, yeah. Freakiest shit ever. I was convinced I was going a bit demon myself, but it seems like when the baby is part-Sombran, that happens. Even when the mother is a demoness." She tilts her head a little, eyeing me closely. "That hasn't happened to you?"

I shake my head.

"Weird. Maybe it's because you're here already. You know, with the clan healer living close by. I stopped by right after the new year so he could look me over, make sure everything's okay. Not like I can see a human doctor on Earth, right? Anyway, Azazel… he's the healer… he made it so my hand stopped turning to shadow on me. It lasted until a couple of days ago, so we came back for a tune-up."

"Azazel," I echo. "I know Azazel. He's the demon who traded a spell from my mate for these little candies for me and, holy shit, they're some kind of demon prenatal vitamin, aren't they?"

Shannon digs into her back pocket, pulling out one. "Depends. This the candy you've been eating?"

I nod.

"He gave these to me, too. I don't know if they're magic or some kind of demon juju, but you're right. They taste pretty good so I eat them, and Azazel said they'll make it easier for me to give birth when the time does come."

That's a small blessing. One of the reasons why I didn't really mind it when I thought that me and Loki couldn't have kids was the lack of any kind of hospital in Nuit. We have a healer but, not gonna lie, the idea of giving birth without an epidural freaked me out a little.

But, unless I'm wrong, Shannon's telling me that the healer is kinda like her demon OB/GYN? Maybe I'm not supposed to worry about that at all.

Small mercy, I guess.

"I still don't get it, though," I admit. "By my calendar, it should be… September? October? And it's—"

"May 25th," Shannon supplies.

"Wow."

"Yup. That's part of living in Sombra for you. Time… it doesn't move the same here as it does back home. Let me guess: every time you see the gold moon, you think it's been another month, right?"

The demons refer to it as a cycle. When I stopped keeping track myself, it made sense to judge time by the appearance of the gold moon. "That's right."

Shannon winces. "Thought so. And, except for me and Mal popping in to see Azazel, there aren't any humans in Nuit. So you wouldn't know."

"I'm beginning to think there's a lot I don't know," I mutter under my breath.

"Well, did you know that one cycle of the gold moon is really closer to three on Earth?"

No. No, I did not.

That explains why Shannon's convinced a year's passed while I was convinced it was, like, October back home. It's not. It really is May again.

Not that it matters. I'm as immortal as Loki. Time doesn't mean anything in a world like this, something I accepted soon after I bonded myself to him.

Shannon gives her hand a flippant wave. "It's alright. After one hell of a case of jet lag, your body will adjust once you take a portal back home again. You'll be fine in no time."

Wait— *what*?

"Home? What do you mean? This is my home."

"Is it? Is it really?"

"Of course it is! Sure, I'm kinda pissed that

everyone had to find out about my baby before me, but I'm not leaving Loki because of it."

"Even if he stole you in the first place?"

Hang on.

How does Shannon know that?

CHAPTER 18
SACRIFICES

KENNEDY

I should've known better. It seems like some things are universal, and despite living in Nuit for… well, I don't know how long exactly, but a while… despite living in Nuit for a while, I'm just figuring out that demons have a tendency to gossip as much as humans do.

How does Shannon know that Loki technically threw me over his shoulder and carried me through a portal in Sombra?

Because I told Lilith that one day when we were chatting about how we met our mates.

I'd thought it was a normal way Sombra males claimed their mates, kind of like the Roman soldiers and the Sabine Women, but Lilith's politely puzzled expression told me I was way off base on that one.

227

I quickly changed the subject that day. We never spoke of it again. I guess I thought the demoness had forgotten all about it.

I would be wrong on that front.

Somehow, after Lilith mentioned to Apollyon about how Loki stole me from my bedroom, the clan leader worried that I had been mated against my will. I'm part of the clan now, regardless of the fact that I'm only here because I came with Loki. An honorable male, Apollyon has a duty to protect me.

And the kind-hearted, well-meaning demon got it in his head that he needed to protect me from my mate by involving Shannon and her mate, Malphas…

"So, the head of this place—"

"Apollyon," I say.

"Right. Him. He asked me to check on you. Make sure you were happy with your mate."

What? I don't understand. Any of the miscommunications we had at the beginning of our mating were all settled before we came to Nuit. Since then, Loki's been the perfect guy—forgetting to mention he knocked me up, withstanding—and I love him.

"Of course I am. Why wouldn't I be? And he didn't steal me. Well, no, he did," I correct. "But that's because he didn't understand why I wouldn't want to go home with him right away."

"Why's that?" asks Shannon. "I asked Mal about him after we left Apollyon's place. If he remembered him. He says that your mate disappeared from Nuit.

That he was lost to the shadows before he turned up with you."

I can't deny that. "He's good to me, Shannon. Really good to me."

"So good you have a cut on your cheek?"

My hand flies to my face. "That was an accident and you know it."

Shannon exhales roughly. "You're right. I do, but if he's anything like my mate, it's like he's programmed to worship you. But it also means he's programmed to be your freaking shadow. You know what I mean, right? Always up your butt... if you want to go back home, you can. Apollyon and Mal will make sure of it."

No. I can't. Loki belongs in Sombra, and I belong with him.

"No, thanks."

"Just think it over. The offer's there. Apollyon already has help from the capital coming in to contain him if you're afraid of him coming after you. When me and Mal go back to Jericho, you could come with us."

From our interactions, I always thought Shannon Crewes was a little flighty, but still pretty smart. Did her big demon mate fuck the sense right out of her? Because I can't understand why a woman who has a Sombra male as her own would ever think I'd be afraid of *mine*—and I tell her so with a huff that has her backing off.

"Hey. Don't shoot the messenger. I'm just repeating what I heard, and rumor's that the demons here all expect him to turn again any day now." She holds up her hands in defense when she sees the furious look on my face. "You gotta admit, he didn't make the best first impression when he was getting ready to charge at Mal and me."

"Loki saw another human and his first reaction was to shield me," I argue. "He thought you were here to take me away from him."

He didn't say so with words. Remembering his emotions rushing through me as he spied Shannon heading toward me, my mate felt a flash of fear, of possession, of love... he saw a human and thought she was there to bring me back to Earth—and he wasn't wrong, was he?

Then again, the knowing look she gives me back says I made her point for her.

Frustration wells up inside of me. She's a human with a demon mate. I thought she'd understand. "It's not how it sounds. He's not keeping me trapped here. I *want* to be with him. Besides, there's nothing back for me in the human world. This is my life now."

"Are you sure about that? What about your family? They must think you've just up and disappeared."

Honestly? They probably didn't even notice.

"Loki's the only family I need."

"And your store? I don't know what kind of deal

you had with your landlord or anything, but it's still there. All the books are inside. You could open it up tomorrow."

I… I *could*?

That store was my life. I loved Turn the Page, and I sacrificed so much for it—

I don't even hesitate. "Or you could."

"What? Kennedy, no. That's not what—"

Too bad. "I mean it. I'm not sure how all the logistics would work or if you'd even want the store, but take it. I'm that sure that I'm staying here. In fact… hang on. Okay?"

I wait for Shannon to nod, then I scoop Freya up, settling her on my seat as I get to my feet. Before Shannon can ask me what I'm doing, I've left the front room, scurrying into the bedroom.

After I explained to him what I wanted, Loki conjured me a bookshelf woven from shadows. I have three treasured books that Lilith gave me perched on the first shelf, and the *Grimoire du Sombra* displayed on the one below it. Grabbing the leather-bound tome, I return to Shannon.

"Here." I offer it to her. "Take this with you."

Shannon crosses her arms over her chest, a small smile on her face. "Fucking hell. I *knew* you had the book all along."

Obviously. How else would I have summoned Loki?

"It worked for me. It worked for you, too. Maybe

there's someone else it's meant to find, and another Sombra demon who's waiting for their mate."

"You're not wrong about that. But... I think you should keep it for now."

"Really? What for?"

"I have my reasons," Shannon says vaguely. "Besides, it's not like I won't have another chance to grab it. If you think Sombra is the place for you, I'll be back before you know it. Can always snag the book then if I have to."

I'm not sure what that means—or why she's refusing to take it now. But if she's backing down on me going back to Jericho with her... I'll take it.

Just in case, I double-check. "Are you sure?"

I expect her to nod. Maybe give me another flippant answer.

She doesn't.

I'm still clutching the book in my hands. Though I'm holding it out to her so she can take it if she changes her mind, Shannon stumbles backward with such force instead, it's like I whacked her with it.

"Shannon?"

She clutches her shoulder, eyes gone wild as she whips her head around. "Mal!"

That's panic in her voice, and fear thinning her lips before she turned her back on me.

My stomach goes tight as I move toward her. "What? What happened? What's going on?"

Shannon is staring at my closed door, almost like she can see through the wood and out into the village if she tries hard enough. "I don't know. It's… I think that was Mal. I think he's hurt. I… shit, Kennedy. I gotta go."

I'm so confused. "Go where?"

"To Mal. Something's wrong."

"But he's with Loki."

The look she throws me over her shoulder as she dashes for the door tells me that she hasn't forgotten that for one second.

"Mal protects me," she says, groping for the door-knob. "And I protect him."

It's a tricky one. Loki conjured one for me when he realized that, with a human mate, the door couldn't just be decorative. I can't zoom out of the ceiling or pass through the door in mist like he can. Shannon got lucky with it earlier; either that, or she's panicking enough now that it's a struggle.

"Give it a jiggle, then a turn and—"

She's got it. Without a second look back at me, she bolts outside.

For a couple of seconds, I stand there, holding the book, trying to make sense of what just happened. Then, reaching out instinctively for Loki, I stumble when I remember that I can't.

Normally, I wouldn't be worried. But Shannon… she can sense her mate while mine is still eerily missing. And it's not just that he's giving me space from him. Unless I'm wrong, it's like our bond has simply disappeared like it never was.

Please, please let me be wrong…

I'd never tested the reach of it before. After our bond was finalized and I didn't have to worry about Loki going up in flames, he never really went far enough away from me that I couldn't sense him if I tried. So unless he left the village center and Shannon's mate lingered, I should be able to know where he is, especially as determined as I am to call him to me.

And I *can't*.

I'm done with sulking. I never should have left him alone in the first place, punishing him for something that had never intended. I don't know what's happening out there, but I'm not going to hide out in our den.

Shannon went off to find her mate just now. It's my turn to do the same.

"Freya, stay," I tell my pet in Sombran.

She chirps, eyes and ears alert as she wraps her fluffy tail around her front paws.

Once I'm sure she'll listen, I take off after Shannon, grimoire and all.

LOKI

True to our nature, Sombra demons shadow their mates. Before a bond is finalized, we must. If we don't, the flames find us, a painful reminder that we have to stay within a certain distance of our mate.

My Kennedy accepted me as her male many cycles ago. She's mine as I am hers, so there is no consequence if I have to leave her to meet with Apollyon or any other villager in need of a spell. But as I sense her nerves—for the first time since I brought her to Sombra with me, I scent her apprehension and feel it pulsing down our bond—and my own heart breaks as hers aches... I nearly got to my knees as I accept that I've sent my mate running from me.

She *runs* from *me*.

And because she made it clear that she needs to put some distance between us, I dig my heels in the ash instead and stay right where she left me.

Because Kennedy... she's gone.

That she fled for the home we share does little to calm me. Never since our bonding has she rejected me—until now. With words, with deed, but more than that, through her essence, she has, and it's all my fault.

Another pang hits me, straight from Kennedy. A touch of hope, a flash of motherly affection toward the spawn she hadn't known about, and then... *betrayal.*

Again, I nearly drop to my knees in agony. They buckle as I swallow the howl burning my throat, gripping my skull between my hands before I shove them away.

It's the betrayal that does it. The thought that she

feels betrayed by her male... by *me*... I'm torn between going to my mate to explain and staying away because that's what she wants.

My Kennedy does not want her male. She believes I lied to her. That I willingly misled her so that I could plant my seed in her, breed her, and have her birth our offspring.

I would never. She must understand that.

Why doesn't she understand?

"Kennedy," I gasp. My chest is heaving. My hands are curled into tight fists now, the points of my claws digging into the flesh. Against my will, I stumble a few steps forward. "Kennedy..."

I hear my name.

Not from my mate. Not her sweet voice, not her sweet scent. Still, I glance up and I find another pair of yellow eyes. Not the artist now, but the clan leader approaches. I see Apollyon with a frown tugging his lips.

But no Kennedy.

Another voice, gruff and masculine, reaches me from behind. I spin and find Malphas easing toward me as if I'm a fierce arkoda about to attack.

A *beast*.

His steps are tentative. Careful.

"Calm yourself," he rumbles. "You wouldn't want your mate to see you like this."

Does he think I do not know that? That I would rather dig my claws into my chest and rip out my own beating heart than believe for a second that I've broken Kennedy's?

The moment the shadows started rising up in me, I closed off our bond so that the madness would not touch her. Even now, I'm grateful she is not here to witness it as go fully demonic once more.

And I have no one else to blame. *I* did this. My intentions are no excuse. She is hurt, and I am lost.

Moving ever closer, Malphas dares to lay his hand on my shoulder. "You must listen, Loki. She deserves an honorable male. She deserves to be with her kin. With her kind."

I know that, too. And I know exactly what the other male is implying with his simple statement.

Jerking away from his friendly touch, I rear a few steps back. He lets me go, believing that I can't stand the heat of his palm against my skin. And while that's so, the rage pulses through me and, as I look at the artist, I don't see the kindness in his yellow eyes.

I only see the male who thinks to come between me and my mate, one way or another.

It never even occurs to me to use magic. Primal and torn, I react with force.

Ducking my head, I slam into Malphas with my two-horns. As two points—the horns on my left side—rip into the bulk of his solid shoulder, Malphas clamps his jaw shut so his mate can't hear him cry out in undeniable pain.

He didn't turn shadow. As though he never

expected me to charge him, he stayed solid as I hit him. And because I *am* shadow, my strike cut him even deeper.

Blood perfumes the air. As if I wasn't already on the cusp of losing my control—or maybe I've already lost it—the scent of demon blood would have been enough to push me over. Throwing back my head, I bare my fangs at Malphas and snarl.

I was once a mage. I wanted to be one again for Kennedy, to be the male worthy of her love and her heart. But a century in the shadows has turned me into the very beast she accused me of being, and as the rage floods my veins, it's like I never left the dark.

Kill.

Tear.

Hunt.

Survive.

I stamp my foot in the ash, the rough pieces cutting past my shadow form and slicing my heel. No matter. Tucking my chin to my chest, showing off my two-horns, I prepare to rush him again when, suddenly, Kennedy's pretty face flashes in front of my eyes.

Like a vision, like a haze, like a phantom, she hovers between Malphas and me.

For her, I am a good male. For her, I am a demon, but not demonic.

For my precious Kennedy, I would pluck the gold moon from the sky with my claws and give it to her, if she'd only ask. I'd turn meat into a pet, I'd leave my sanctuary in the shadows to rejoin the village, and I'd do anything and everything for my female.

She is my heart beating outside of my chest, and the only thing that can battle the shadows threatening to take me over completely. I'd never task her with that—it isn't fair to put my sanity in her dainty little hands—but while my tempestuous mate will forgive me for assuming she knew she was carrying out spawn, I know her inside and out.

She will never forgive me if I go fully demonic again.

Because as I would lose her, she would lose me. There are depths to the shadows that my human mate cannot follow me to, and while our mate bond saved me once, once was all I get.

If I had to go through the pain of losing her, I would if it pleased Kennedy. But I will never put her through the same, no matter what it costs me.

Even if it costs me her anyway...

A howl erupts from my throat. Digging in my heels, I straighten, twisting so that my horns aren't angled at anyone. Not Malphas. Not Apollyon. Not—

Glaine.

It's the green eyes that give him away. I met him centuries ago in Marvo, when I was first brought to the School of Mages. Duke Haures's lead guard and soldier, everyone in Sombra knows of him.

If he's here in Nuit, it's most certainly on the duke's orders.

And next to him, stepping out of a portal, the golden runes running down his inky black, shadowy arms, is a male I haven't seen in a hundred years.

Sammael. My friend. My mentor.

Purple eyes—mage eyes—gleam out of his shadowy face as the portal closes behind him. "Loki. It is time."

The sharp tone is familiar. It's not Kennedy, so I don't want to listen, but at the same time, it demands me to obey.

If only I had the last time I faced him.

In between his hands, he's conjured a length of golden chain, glowing brightly. Powerful enough to contain an unbonded demon and his essence, Sammael has thrown all of his might behind enchanting this set before passing them off to the duke's soldier.

Good. Because I feel the rage returning, and the only thing that shall save my Kennedy from any more pain is that chain.

And every demon gathered in the square knows it.

Straight-backed and proud, I shake my head, showing off my set of double horns. And then, for my heart, for my *family*, I hold out my hands and allow Glaine to slap the manacles on the wrists of my shadow form.

CHAPTER 19
LILITH SAVES LOKI

KENNEDY

When I dash into the village square and see that Loki's hands are in front of him, a length of brilliant gold chains connecting his wrists, I almost lose my fucking mind.

He's not alone. Since I left him with Mal, a small crowd has formed. I see Apollyon, Mal and Shannon, a few villagers on the edge of the square, and two males flanking my mate.

Both of them are in their shadowy forms. They're the only ones. One of them has purple eyes, like Loki; the other's glow a vivid green.

A jolt slams into me, one of Loki's memories slipping out past the shadows concealing most of his. The male with the purple eyes is Sammael, the duke's personal mage and Loki's former mentor. The green-eyed demon is Glaine, the duke's pet soldier.

When Duke Haures takes a prisoner, these are the two demons he sends. Sammael forges the chain. Glaine enforces the duke's will, bringing his charge to stand before the demon Duke of Sombra.

And now they've come for Loki.

"No!"

Loki's head jerks up. His purple eyes are a dimmer shade than usual. Because of the chains, I realize. There's magic in the links and they're doing something to weaken him.

"Kennedy," he whispers. "Go."

As if.

"What's going on? Loki, why are you wearing chains?"

He doesn't answer me. No one does.

At least, not yet.

Now, I arrived only seconds after Shannon did. While I'm gaping at the chains, she's running her hands over her mate's bulk.

That's when I notice the blood shimmering from a set of puncture wounds and tears in his shoulder. As red as his skin, I only see it because it *does* shimmer.

Furious, she jerks her bloody thumb at Loki. "Did he do that to you, Mal? 'Cause I'm about to kick his ass if he did."

"Do not worry about me, my mate."

Malphas goes from his demon form to his shadows, then back again. He's completely healed, no sign of the puncture wounds left on his tattooed chest.

She sniffs. "Fine. But I don't care. Chains or no chains, I can take him."

No, she couldn't. Especially if my mate lost enough control that he gored his fellow demon, he would've made mincemeat of her. Up until now, I never would've thought him possible of that—but I saw the puncture wounds before they vanished. There were two distinct holes, one for each of the horns on one side of his head.

Is that why he's chained? Did he turn on Malphas and the duke's guards came for him?

No. *No.* A combination of Loki's recent memories and a hint of his scattered emotions finding their way to me through the whisper of our bond—plus Shannon's earlier comment—makes me realize what must have happened.

The guards were already here. To keep Loki contained in case I wanted to leave with Shannon and Mal and my mate wouldn't willingly let me. He must have snapped a little, attacking the other demon male, and the guards took the chance to chain him up.

And that's when Glaine basically confirms my suspicion when he says, "He's a danger to all of demonkind. Anyone who is fully demonic must be executed."

"But he survived the shadows," Apollyon tells Glaine. "If you banish him there, what then?"

Glaine's green eyes glitter. "Duke Haures has other ways to punish rogues."

Executed.

Punished.

No!

I dash in front of Loki.

I know how silly I look. These demons dwarf me, I'm still clutching the grimoire, but I couldn't care less. This is my mate. If they want us to go back to the shadows, that's fine. We can do that. We were happy there before, and we can be happy there again.

But *executed?*

"You can't do that."

Glaine gives me a look of barely concealed annoyance. "Who are you?"

I wave wildly behind me, gesturing at the tattoo of my name on his chest, written in Sombran runes. "His mate."

"Impossible," sniffs the solider. "Rogues cannot take mates. Once lost, there's no essence for the exchange."

"Bullshit. I have his essence, *Glaine.*" Breathing heavy, panicking more than I want to, I pause a moment to let that sink in. When the ridges over his long nose draw together, I know I made my point. "See? How else would I know who you are? Or that Sammael is Loki's former teacher? I have his essence and I made the mate's promise. If that means he's not rogue, he's not rogue. 'Cause he's not, okay? Now let my mate go!"

"The duke—"

Screw the duke. "He didn't do anything wrong!"

"Uh, Kennedy—"

I whirl on Shannon. I can only imagine what my face looks like because she holds up her hands again. "Never mind."

Okay, so maybe Loki attacked her mate; I can't deny that. But Malphas is immortal, and my mate was upset after I walked away from him, and he got the idea that Shannon and her mate were here to separate us. All of that pops right into my head at the same time, more proof that Loki's essence is still inside of me.

Rogue, my ass. He's protective and he's devoted and he's *mine*—and I'll make sure everyone of these demons know it.

In my fiercest voice, I demand, "Take those chains off of him. Now."

Glaine sticks out his chin. "And if I don't?"

I don't know what I'll do, but I'm saved from having to bluff when I hear another familiar voice.

"This is ridiculous," calls out Lilith. She appears on the edge of the square, walking regally toward us as she addresses Apollyon. "Mate, what is going on here? Why are these Sombran guards in our village? There's no need for this."

"There was a worry that Loki might go fully

demonic again, Lilith, my love. He challenged Malphas. He started to turn. I have to protect the rest of Nuit."

She scoffs. "Turn? Are you going blind in your old age, my mate? Because he has a mage's eyes, not the white of a rogue."

Lilith is right. Peering up at him to double-check, I see that his eyes are still purple.

"They've been purple since the night he gave me his essence," I blurt out. "Since we bonded."

"See? And unless demons butting horns in a chain offense, I cannot imagine why the poor soul is still wearing them. Glaine, take them off."

"Lilith—"

"Glaine. Remove them."

To my absolute amazement, he nods at Sammael. "You heard the clanmother. The charge is that Loki is a rogue. He might have been once. He's not now. Remove the chains, Sammael."

The mage doesn't make any visible reaction. Expression guarded, he waves his hand.

The moment the cuffs are off, Loki bounds over to me. He wraps me up in his arms, lifting me off the ground as he rubs his cheek against mine. Love floods me: love for my mate, and the love my mate has for me.

"My heart, my mate, my Kennedy." His voice is a hot whisper in my ear. "If I had known you didn't, I would've told you. I'm so sorry. Please forgive me."

I already have. "It's okay. Everything's going to be okay."

At least, it *better* be.

Once Loki sets me back down, reluctantly releasing me, I glare at the crowd gathered. Apollyon has the good sense to look sheepish, Lilith is proud, Glaine is sneaking peeks at the Soleil demoness, Shannon is clinging to Mal, and Sammael just looks bored now.

"Come, Glaine," he says. "The duke will want to hear about this."

The green-eyed demon gives Lilith one last curious look before nodding. "Yes. I guess you're right." He turns to the clan leader. "Apollyon. I trust you to let us know if we're needed again."

"Of course."

Lilith sidles over to her mate, taking his claw-tipped hand in one of her daintier ones. "As always, a pleasure, Glaine."

Surprisingly, the soldier's expression softens. "Regardless of the circumstances, it was good seeing you again, Lilith." Turning back to Sammael, he jerks his head. "Prepare another portal. It'll be faster."

Once the portal winks out, taking the soldier and the mage with it, the square goes quiet. Every single one of the villagers gathered is watching Loki and me as though expecting his eyes to go from purple to white, and for him to go on a rampage.

But he won't. I know my mate. The shadows are strong, but he's stronger.

With me by his side, he'll never go rogue again.

"ON THAT NOTE," ANNOUNCES SHANNON WHEN THE quiet becomes too noticeable, "we're gonna be heading out, too. But, first, does anyone got a pen?"

The demons on the edge of the square—plus Apollyon—all look confusedly at each other. Probably because 'pen' doesn't have a direct translation in Sombran, so while I understand what she's looking for, no one else does.

Except for Lilith.

"Would an ash stick work for you? I use it for lessons."

"Maybe. What do you got? Can I see?"

Reaching into the brown and yellow dress she's wearing, Lilith pulls out something that looks more like a used matchstick to me. A wooden base with a black tip, ashy like a struck match made up of embers, it's about the size of Lilith's pointer finger.

In Shannon's grip, it looks pretty much like a pencil.

She grins at Lilith. "Perfect. Thanks." With a grabby motion, she gestures at the book I'm still holding.

What? "I thought you said for me to hang onto this?"

"I did. You should. But I just want to see the inner cover of the book real quick. Okay?"

If she says so. With a shrug, I pass it over.

"Mal, babe? Come here."

"As you wish," rumbles her besotted mate.

I'm glad they're seem to be so happy together. Occasionally I would think of Shannon and how she had the book before me. I'd wonder if she found her true love, and if she did, I couldn't help but would if he was a Sombra demon, too. I knew the answer from the moment I saw the two walking toward me and Loki in the village square, but with everything else that's happened, I haven't gotten the chance to ask her about her experience with the spellbook—and her feelings for her mate.

I don't have to to guess that they're as perfectly matched as me and Loki. She's obviously fiercely protective of a demon two heads taller than her, and every time Mal glances down at her, you almost expect little red hearts to replace his gleaming, gold-colored eyes.

Shannon motions for him to stand in front of her. "Give me your back, 'kay? I need something hard to write on."

He does. Hefting the book up, she flips open the front cover.

I know what it says. I've read the *Grimoire du Sombra* front to back so many times that I can probably recite a couple of the epic Sombra poems detailed in there. On the front cover, there are two names written inside. I never really paid much attention to them. When I ran Turn the Page, most used books came in with the names of their previous owners scrawled on the inner cover.

Looking back, I probably should've questioned that more. I might be the only human woman who lives in Nuit, but seeing Shannon is proof that I'm not the only human mate for one of these demons.

Hm. I wonder how many of us there are?

Even better question: what is Shannon doing?

She rests the book against the small of Mal's back, bowing her head over the book so that she can write on the inner cover.

"Something I meant to do before it went missing." Glancing over at me, Shannon winks, then finishes what she's doing. After sparing a quick squeeze to Mal's side and a murmured 'thank you', she lifts up the book so I can see what she did.

Written in all caps, she's added: **SHANNON CREWES** beneath the other two names that were already there.

Then, her grin turning mischievous, she holds the stick out to me. "Your turn."

"Do I want to know why we're writing our names in this book?" I ask, taking the stick as she moves the book in front of me next.

250

"Probably not. But since I'm going to tell you anyway… think of it as a library book. Everyone who checks the book out and gets their demon leaves their name behind. Susanna Benoit was first," Shannon says, pointing to the script at the top. "Then Amy—"

The first name is written in script. *Susanna M. Benoit*. After comparing the handwriting to the additions to the **VERUS AMOR** page, I decided ages ago that the mysterious Susanna was responsible for the translations.

The second name, however, is a childish scrawl. I just assumed it was a kid in Susanna's family who added their name—and that's why I'm slightly taken aback when Shannon mentions that *Amy* also has a demon of her own back on Earth.

"Can't help but notice that Amy looks like she was maybe seven," I point out.

"Nine," Shannon corrects.

I nearly choke. I was being facetious, but she's dead serious. "Did you say *nine*?"

"Yup." At my look of horror, Shannon waves her hand absently. "It's not what you think. Amy summoned her mate when she was a kid, but they didn't actually bond until she was in her mid-twenties."

With a glance back over to where Loki is basically vibrating in place, his need to touch me, to hold me, to *love* me so strong it's spilling out of his big body, she adds almost conversationally, "Nox was in the duke's dungeon until then, wearing chains just like his. It was a lot harder for him to get out of them than your beast."

He's not my beast. Not anymore. He's my mate, and I'm not going to let anyone cage him—or chain him—while I'm around.

Sending a message to Loki that I'm just about done, I place the stick to the page as Shannon holds it for me. I smudge the **K** because I'm not used to writing with this type of pencil, but the rest of my name comes out pretty decent. Following Shannon's lead, I add **Barnes** next to it.

She nods in approval, easing the front cover closed before she hands it back to me. "Good. Now the next chick who finds it won't think she's alone."

I'm about to ask Shannon if she's so sure that someone else will when I realize that that's a ridiculous question. I did, didn't I?

And before me, Shannon did. So did Amy, and Susanna, too.

Hugging the book to my chest, I wonder who will be next—especially since the book's sticking around Nuit for a little bit longer.

Shannon gives me a knowing nod. Then, patting her big demon on the back, she says, "Well, now that that's all settled, what do you say? Ready to go home?"

If her mate is anything like mine, when Mal's eyes

light up, he's already imagining Shannon half-naked. "I can summon the portal back right now."

His eyes aren't purple. He's not a mage like Loki is, though he doesn't have to be. With a human as his mate, Mal would've been able to rip a hole between worlds after the first time Shannon called him to her.

Loki explained that to me. Just like there was a reason he stole me to Sombra once he knew he was my mate, it's the same for why he can't send me back to Earth. Because while he *could* bring me home, if anyone but me ever laid eyes on him in the human world, we would be breaking Duke Haures's first law. That might mean chains, or it could mean death, depending on the ruthless ruler's mood.

And, no matter what, Loki will never risk me— and once I understood that, I decided I'd rather be with Loki in his world than without him in mine.

I wouldn't risk him, either, though I do have to wonder what it's like to be a Sombra demon's mate in the human world. To never be able to announce proudly that he's yours, to have to hide in the shadows with him so no one would learn demons exist. It can't be easy, and I have to admit that I made the best decision staying here and sticking by it. In Sombra, I'll never have to hide.

It's definitely better this way, even if there are things I miss about my old life...

While Mal's arms start to glow with the same golden runes as Sammael's, building a portal to Earth beside his human mate, Shannon turns and waves at me and Loki. "See you soon, guys."

I moved toward her. "Shannon, wait."

She cocks her head, curious. "Yeah?"

"Sorry about stealing the book. I just… I had to. You understand that, right?"

Shannon glances up at her mate, narrow face full of love and affection as she meets his golden gaze. "Oh, yeah. I got you. And no worries. That book always seems to find someone who's fated for one of these guys. If you didn't sell it to me, who knows? Maybe I would've been the one to steal it from you."

Put like that, she has a point. "One more thing. You said 'soon'… that means you're going to be coming back, right?"

"Yup. Every couple of cycles until I'm ready to pop," she confirms. "Me and Mal, we're gonna stick it out in the human world for a bit longer, but when this little guy or gal comes, we're thinking about having a long vacation here in Sombra." She snorts. "Can you imagine going into labor in a human hospital? Nah. Azazel's gonna help me through it."

That's just what I was hoping to hear. The idea that I'm pregnant—while exciting—isn't as daunting when I know I'm not going to be the only human woman with a demon baby.

I can't go back home. For so many reasons—not the least of all that Loki might just lose his shit again if I so much as suggested a quick pop into the human world right now—it's better if I continue to go all in on my life here in Sombra.

But if Shannon has no problem coming and going…

"Great. But could I ask you a favor?"

Her eyes twinkle. "Hey, you gave me your store. Do you know how much I'd rather sell books than push paper products for a corporation for a living? I'm a kickass salesperson but I think it's time to be my own boss… at least until the baby's here. Shoot, Kennedy. Whatever favor you want, it's yours."

In that case—

"When you come back, do you think you could bring me my Kindle?"

Shannon blinks. "You mean your e-reader?"

That's right. I nod just a touch sheepishly. "I miss my books."

"Girl, you got it. And I'm so glad you said that. I'm already thinking about all the things I'm gonna bring when we come back, and I would've totally blanked on mine. I'll even do you one better and make sure all the books you have are downloaded on the device before we cross over." She grins. "We can have our own Sombra book club, and when the battery dies, I'll pop back home for a charge."

Yes!

I launch myself at the blonde, wrapping my arms around her. "Thank you, Shannon."

She squeezes me back. "Don't mention it. Us

mates have got to stick together. I'm just glad you're happy and safe."

Releasing her, I immediately go right back to my demon mate. Ducking under his arm, letting it settle possessively over my shoulder as I lean into Loki, I smile at my former customer—and new friend.

Sending a pulse of pure love down to my mate, I snuggle up next to him.

"I am," I promise. "I really am."

EPILOGUE

KENNEDY

Thanks to Loki's essence, I know enough about the formidable Duke Haures that the ruler of Sombra wasn't going to be too happy when his soldier and his mage went back without their prisoner.

I stand by what I said. If everyone was worried that Loki was going to go fully demonic again, he proved them all wrong. Now, I'm not gonna lie and say that he didn't get *close*—and I'm not sure Shannon's ever going to really forgive him for using his horns against her mate even if Mal was a good sport about it—but emotions were high all around.

I just found out I was pregnant, Loki was afraid—and for good reason, too—that Shannon's arrival in

Nuit meant it was time for me to leave, and the other bonded couple was just trying to help.

Apollyon and Lilith, too. After Shannon and Mal took a portal back to Jericho, I grabbed Loki by the hand and dragged my mate home with me before anyone else could try to come between us. We had a lot to talk about together, and still bristling from the fear he had lost me, Loki had something to prove to me in bed, but when we eventually left our house, Apollyon invited us to dinner with him and his mate.

Shannon was right. Lilith didn't want to upset me with the rumors running rampant in Nuit. Like everyone else, she also knew about my bun in the oven, but didn't say anything out of respect for our cultural differences. In Soleil—like in Sombra—a woman didn't celebrate until she gave birth. Assuming humans were the same, she was saving her congratulations for then. With this being mine and Loki's first offspring, she didn't want me to hear how most of the other villagers were placing coin wagers on how long before his eyes went white again as the shadows took him over again.

That pissed me off way more than the miscommunication about me being pregnant did. So many of our so-called clansmen were happy to let him use his magic to help them out while they were talking shit behind his back.

I can't stop myself from holding a bit of a grudge against them. I now understand why Shannon is so fiercely protective of her Malphas. Loki is a foot and a half taller than I am, he has four horns, plus claws that would put a knife to shame… and I still feel like he needs me to stick up for him.

If I have to go up on my tiptoes, grab him by his chin, kiss him in front of all of Nuit to show them that I'm not afraid before pointing at his purple eyes and resisting the urge to stick out my tongue at the villagers… and failing… damn right I will. And I do, with Lilith standing near enough by me that none of the clan will go against the clanmother.

Beast or mage, male or monster, Loki is mine, and if they don't like it, I'll go back to the shadows with him if I have to.

He's my mate. I'll go with him anywhere.

Including to Marvo when our presence is requested in the duke's palace.

It might be a request, but the green-eyed soldier makes it clear that it's one we can't refuse. And that's how, a few days after things have settled down in the village, Glaine appears with a summons to meet the duke.

Nuit reminds me of Hell. No getting around that. With the ash fields, the red sky, the *heat*… throw in a couple of flames, and it earns the distinction of being a demon village. The skulls on the edge of the shadows help sell the image, too.

Marvo, on the other hand, is an absolute oasis. Just like how the moon is red in Nuit and black in the shadows, it's a soft blue in Marvo. The temperature reminds me of a spring day in New York. It smells of flowers instead of rotten eggs, and the orb lights flickering around the palace leave a blue tint on everything. In every way, it's the complete opposite of our village, down to the male looming impressively on his throne.

It's one thing to know that Duke Haures is unique of all Sombra demons. His eyes are the same bluish shade as the flickering lights in his throne room, and instead of having red skin in his demon form, it's as white as freaking snow. Of course, the light tinges his pale skin, reflecting off his white horns, coloring the throne nestled between them.

He's bigger, too. With a set of fangs that grow up from the bottom, his face is more monstrous. And yet, when he calls us to stand before his throne, his voice is nowhere near the snarl I expect from him. It's almost gentile, and something about his tone has my legs itching to drop down into a curtsy.

Loki and I were escorted to Marvo by Glaine. Once the portal brought us to the duke's palace, he vanished into the shadows.

That doesn't mean that we face Duke Haures alone.

On the contrary. There are two other demons standing near the throne: one to the right of it, one standing just behind it. I've seen the male with the purple eyes before: Sammael, the mage who conjured the chains for my mate.

Doesn't matter that Loki's essence tells me he's a lot more than that. He put chains on Loki. I hate him on principle.

The other male is almost as unique to me as the duke is. Tall with a lankier build, he wears his black hair shorter than most demons; it's wild and just about hits his hard jaw. That's not so unusual, but his vivid red eyes? A glowing beacon that make his demon skin seem like the color of rust in comparison? Those *are*.

Loki knows who he is. Nox was a fierce hunter who stalked along the shadows at the edge of Sombra, providing meat to the villagers of Nuit. Even when Loki lived in the darkness, he would sometimes see Nox's glowing red eyes and remember that he wasn't entirely alone.

But Nox was gone when we left the shadows for the village, and Loki assumed the hunter had simply moved on to another clan.

Yeah. Considering he's hovering over the human woman standing directly in front of him, his hands possessively resting on her shoulders, I think I have a pretty good idea where he went.

And who the woman might be.

I'd put her at a decade younger than me. Twenty-four, maybe twenty-five, though I know better than to think she's actually that young; I can still remember the shock I felt when I plucked Loki's age out of his head, and since she has to be Nox's mate, she would be immortal. Her face is both round and inviting, her brown eyes kind, her lips curved in a friendly smile. She has her rich brown hair pulled over one shoulder, giving me a peek at her mate's chest.

He has a similar marking there. The demon brand, spelling out her name. It's the latter half, though, and the only letter I can translate from this distance is the last one: **A**.

Nox grumbles low in his chest. In the blink of an eye, he goes from his red-skinned demon form to a barely-there shadow and back. The only constants are the patches of black that circle both of his wrists and his intimidating red gaze.

I don't think he likes the way I'm scrutinizing his mate or his chest because, one thing for sure, I know a possessive Sombra demon male when I see one.

Just in case I'm way off base, I point at her with my free hand and say, "Amy or Susanna?"

She blinks back a look of surprise. "Amy. Well, Amelia, but yes. That's me."

That's what I thought. As brawny as her mate is, it didn't look like he has eight letters carved into his skin. "Kennedy. Hi."

"Very astute," observes Duke Haures.

Astute nothing. Flipping open the cover on the book I'm holding, I show them the inside cover with four names, including the childish scrawl that says *Amy*.

"Fifty-fifty odds since I know she's not Shannon. Besides, your guard said to bring the book. Shannon said someone would probably be asking about it. There's only four names in here so, yeah. Now I just have to meet Susanna someday and I'll have met all the human woman and their mates."

"I wish you luck on that," Duke Haures says carefully, "but that's not what I called you here for."

I take a deep breath. "If this is about what happened at the village, I'd just like to point out that Loki's eyes are purple. Okay? Demon, not demonic. We're good."

The duke nods his head solemnly. "I've been briefed on that. All witnesses agree that while your mate could have had a better handle on his rage, he is no more dangerous than Nox here."

Okay. That went a lot better than I was expecting it to. From the relief filtering through my bond with Loki, I'd say he agrees.

The duke chuckles. It's a surprisingly nice sound. "You are young, human. You will learn. We are Sombra demons. Honorable, proud, and protective, especially of our mates. We are also immortal. Who of us hasn't taken a horn to the chest in a battle we should have won? Loki is a two-horn. Powerful, but also quick to act. Possessive, too. It's in his nature as ruling Sombra ruthlessly is mine."

See, now, I was liking how that was going until he got to the 'ruthlessly' part.

Any of the bravado I worked up when I saw another human here disappears as Duke Haures's pale blue eyes shine down on me.

Loki takes one step forward, shifting his bulk so that he's inserted himself between me and the duke.

He notices, too.

"Be at ease, Loki. You wear your female's name on your skin, and its brand on your heart. She is yours. I'll make that plain, but it isn't your mating that interests me. It's the book your mate is clutching in her hands."

Why am I not surprised that, once again, everything comes down to this spellbook?

"You want it? It's yours." And I won't even charge him any coin for it. My bookselling days are over, and I'm thinking it's probably a good idea to get on the right side of the Sombra ruler.

But then he snorts. "What would I do with it? I have a mate of my own and no need for its magic."

Oh. "Okay. I mean, I can bring it back to Nuit if you want. I just… that Glaine guy said to grab it before we left."

"Yes. Because it doesn't belong in Sombra."

I figured. That's why I tried to give it to Shannon before she left. She made it seem like someone else would take care of it, and seeing Nox and Amy standing near the duke, I'm beginning to think I know exactly who that is.

Leaning forward on his throne, Duke Haures explains:

"For two thousand years, I fought to keep Sombra separate from the human world. I don't know how the grimoire found its way to Earth in the first place, but if it hadn't, three of my demons would never have found their human mates. How many more are meant for your people? The only way to know that is to release the grimoire back into your plane.

"Of course, my first law still stands." The law that says humans aren't allowed to know about Sombra. "I won't welcome just any humans into my realm. Only those who take a Sombra demon as their mate like my — like Amelia." The duke gestures toward Amy with one of his claws. "After discussing it, she offered to bring it back with her. Its place is in their world, not ours."

Amy nods. "I can't explain it, but Duke Haures is right. As long as it's in our world... the human world, I mean... somehow that book always ends up finding its way to someone who is fated to love a Sombra demon." She glances up, tilting her head just enough to meet her mate's gaze. "Right, baby?"

"My reason," he murmurs, bending his neck, nuzzling the side of her head with his chin.

Loki reaches behind him, trailing one claw down

my hip. Like he can't help but touch me while the other couple is lost in each other.

And that's when Sammael finally speaks up. "It's magic."

To be honest, I kind of forgot he was there.

"He's right. It is magic," Loki agrees. "Old magic, lost to our mages, but magic all the same, my heart. Just human magic now. It belongs in the human realm." And then, because this Loki after all, he says, "As you belong with me and our family."

Our family. Made up of a beastly demon, a human with a temper, a baby that will be a mix of both of us, and a chittering creature that I'm still convinced is half squirrel, half cat.

I tap the back of the book with my fingernail.

Human magic, huh? He's not wrong. Maybe I thought the 'true love' spell inside of it was a dud at first, but there's no denying it gave me exactly what it promised when Loki finally found me.

My true love, and a happily ever after.

"I assume you're staying in Sombra?" asks the duke. "So you won't need the grimoire anymore."

I think I knew from the moment Loki picked me up and tossed me over his shoulder like some kind of beastly caveman that I would never be going back to Earth again. And while I wouldn't say 'no' if I could hop a portal just to get some things that remind me of home, that could be another one of my infrequent vacations.

This is my *home*.

I did my best to explain that to Shannon, and I made sure the duke's henchmen got the hint.

And now it's Duke Haures's turn to hear it.

"I got what I wanted." Reaching for his big hand, I wrap my fingers around two of Loki's. "And I dare anyone to take him from me."

"Fierce little human. So tiny yet so bold."

The fact that the duke has a reputation for being responsible for so many horned skulls dotting the edge of Sombra's shadows is the only reason I swallow back my heated retort.

That, and the way Loki puffs out his marked chest in pride as he says, "And she is *my* mate."

I don't know why Loki's mentor catches my attention in that moment. I was just about to walk over to Amy so that I could hand her the book—and possibly risk my head and Loki's sanity if I triggered her scowly mate's protective instincts—when my eyes flicker just beyond Duke Haures. They land on Sammael, and I freeze when I see his face.

That's… that's not jealousy on his demon features or barely concealed annoyance, or even boredom like the last time we met.

That's *longing*.

And he's wearing that expression as he stares at the book I'm still holding…

THAT'S IT FOR KENNEDY AND LOKI (FOR NOW, AT least)! But that doesn't mean that's it for Sombra. With the book being passed off to Amy so that another human woman can find her forever with one of these males, I'm happy to announce that the fourth book, *Fated to the Phantom*, will be out this fall! Specifically on Halloween, though *Drawn to the Demon Duke* will start being serialized in April. Make sure to sign up for my newsletter so that you can get weekly installments of Susanna and Haures's story for absolutely free—and keep reading for a sneak peek at Hope and Sammael!

PRE-ORDER NOW

FATED TO THE PHANTOM

I think I'm being haunted... and it's all that weird book's fault.

I'm a librarian. I *love* books.

But the one I found in the depository?

Yeah... there's something off about that one—and not only because I had a hard time figuring out if I should shelve it under foreign, occult, fiction, or out of print selections. I think... I think it's *following* me.

Does that sound crazy? It might. With my anxiety ratcheting up to eleven after a recent rush of break-ins near my house, I'm more on guard than usual. But robbers usually steal stuff, right? They don't snatch library books and plant them in the librarian's home.

And yet, somehow, that's where I find the book.

That's not the only strange thing that's happening to me. I get this feeling like I'm being followed, but when I look behind me, all I see are shadows. I swear I hear a voice calling to me, too…

Okay. Maybe I am going crazy, but when I finally discover that I'm being haunted by a towering shadow monster with horns and a mournful gaze, I decide it's not so bad.

Especially when he finally finds a way to let me know that I'm his fated mate… and he's mine.

Fated to the Phantom is the fourth book in the **Sombra Demons** series. It tells the story of Hope and Sammael, an anxious librarian and the mage-turned-phantom who is trying to catch her attention—and her heart.

Releasing October 31, 2023!

COMING SOON

DRAWN TO THE DEMON DUKE

I spent years trying to decipher the old spellbook I found... and I was drawn to the duke in seconds.

I found the book in a library when I was sixteen. For the next twelve years, I made it my purpose to figure out what it was about. I'd always been interested in languages, and it amazed me that this wasn't any one I could research about.

Until I figured out that it wasn't just one language. It had its roots in Latin, with at least five other languages thrown in the mix, and once I saw the pattern, it was easy to translate the rest.

I already knew it was a spellbook. The title —*Grimoire du Sombra*—gave it away. But what I didn't know? Was that, after reading the whole book, I'd find a true love spell… and that it would work.

I took all of the precautions. Probably more than I needed to, but it didn't matter. When the portal opened in my living room, showing me a realm that shouldn't exist, the most awe-inspiring creature I'd ever seen strode into my room.

Duke Haures, the rule of Sombra—and, I discover, my fated mate.

Only… I'm human. His first law prevents humans from having any contact with demonkind in his realm. So what is he to do?

If your answer is to use magic to bring me back to Sombra with him, you're exactly right… and, before long, I'm more than happy to stay.

---

* *Drawn to the Demon Duke* is a prequel to the **Sombra Demons** series. It tells the story of Susanna, Amy's aunt, and how she became Duke Haures's best-kept secret.

Make sure to join my newsletter to learn more about this special prequel that will be serialized in weekly installments via my newsletter—for completely free!

KEEP IN TOUCH

Stay tuned for what's coming up next! Visit my site to follow me at any of the places below—or sign up for my newsletter—for news, promotions, upcoming releases, and more!

SARAHSPADEBOOKS.COM

ALSO BY SARAH SPADE

Holiday Hunk

Halloween Boo

This Christmas

Auld Lang Mine

I'm With Cupid

Getting Lucky

When Sparks Fly

Holiday Hunk: the Complete Series

Claws and Fangs

Leave Janelle

Never His Mate

Always Her Mate

Forever Mates

Hint of Her Blood

Taste of His Skin

Stay With Me

Never Say Never: Gem & Ryker

Sombra Demons

Drawn to the Demon Duke*

Mated to the Monster

Stolen by the Shadows

Santa Claws

Bonded to the Beast

Fated to the Phantom

Stolen Mates

The Feral's Captive

Chase and the Chains

The Beta's Bride

Wolves of Winter Creek

Prey

Pack

Predator

Claws Clause

(written as Jessica Lynch)

Mates *free*

Hungry Like a Wolf

Of Mistletoe and Mating

No Way

Season of the Witch

Rogue